You've connected.

danger.com

@5//Stalker/

First Aladdin Paperbacks edition February 1998

Copyright © 1998 by Jordan Cray

Aladdin Paperbacks
An imprint of Simon & Schuster
Children's Publishing Division
1230 Avenue of the Americas
New York, NY 10020

Library of Congress Cataloging-in-Publication Data
Cray, Jordan.
Stalker / by Jordan Cray. — 1st Aladdin Paperbacks ed.
p.   cm. — (Danger.com ; 5)
Summary: After telling her former best friend Mina that she has met a man on the Internet and has been chatting online with him, seventeen-year-old Camille disappears, leaving Mina to suspect foul play.
ISBN 0-689-81476-3
[1. Missing persons—Fiction. 2. Stalking—Fiction.
3. Internet (Computer network)—Fiction. 4. Computers—Fiction. 5. Mystery and detective stories.] I. Title. II. Series:
Cray, Jordan. Danger.com ; 5
PZ7.C85955St   1998
[Fic]—dc21   97-30888
CIP AC

danger.com

@5//Stalker/

by
jordan.cray

Aladdin Paperbacks

//prologue

e–mail communication
TO: MOONSTRK (Deva Winter)
FROM: BIGFAN#1
DATE: April 3
RE: Hello!

You're probably surprised to hear from me, right? You changed your e-mail address again. But I know everything about you. I know that Deva is a moon goddess in Sanskrit. You said that in that article in Le Style *magazine. I like your new e-mail address. Moonstruck.*

Don't be scared, Deva. I just want to be your friend. Your best friend. I know you don't have one. Remember that interview you gave to Celebrity *magazine, when you said it's hard for you to make friends because you're a movie star?*

I would understand when you were tired. Or if you had to cancel. I'm in show business, too. I mean, I was. But I got out of it, because Deva, I know just how hard a business it is. People can say whatever they want about you, and you just have to stand there. Like a piece of meat, downgraded from Grade A Prime to dog food, just because you put on a pound, or have a zit.

You see how I understand? That's what I wanted to say to you in court yesterday. But all those lawyers were around you. You looked so scared. Your lawyers are lying to you, Deva. They're saying I'm dangerous, but it's not true. I don't need to be "restrained." I'm the one who wants to take care of you.

I just want to be friends. Why is that so wrong? That's why I did what I did. I'm sorry you got hurt. It wasn't my fault. If you just hadn't been so scared, you wouldn't have gotten hurt.

Remember in Two of Hearts *how Andrew never gave up on you? He just knew that you'd love him in the end, and you did!*

That's my favorite movie of yours because it's so real. Don't you see, I know we will be friends. I won't give up on you, either.

I'll wait until you're alone, because then, no one can come between us.

Your Number One Fan

e-mail communication
TO: RAPnzl (Dcva Winter)
FROM: BIGFAN#1
DATE: May 10
RE: Ever After

A few nights in jail weren't so scary. And your lawyer didn't scare me, either, Deva. You probably don't know this, but he's paying me money to go away. And the cops have been so mean, too. So I'm going. I wanted to say good-bye. Not for forever—I know we'll be best friends one day.

If you didn't get scared, and scream, things would have worked out. Maybe I just need to give you some time. Maybe I need to prove to you how I can take care of my friends.

I'm going away, Rapunzel. You see how well I know you? I know that you decided to become an actress when you played Rapunzel in second grade! All your e-mail addresses are so easy to figure out.

You shouldn't have rejected me like that. And you shouldn't have screamed. Now I have to find someone else. Someone to watch over, someone to take care of. Like I would for you. Then you'll see.

But don't be jealous. She'll be just like you, but she could never really take your place.

Your Number One Fan

Retrieve: a://nolife.
(Journal of Mina Sterling Kurtz)
april 21

Why would someone who needs to get a life decide to keep a journal? Like I'd ever want to go back and read my 101 complaints about trig, or how seriously strange it is to live in the heart of the decaying infrastructure of the formerly industrial Northeast— otherwise known as my hometown, Mohawk Falls, in Upstate New York.

But today, I've got something to say. Sort of. Camy called and asked me if I wanted to hang out at the mall this afternoon. I looked around, just to see if the moon had turned into blue cheese. But it was daylight. The sun was still up there, sending down some watery spring rays. I said sure.

Don't think for a minute that I don't realize that this is a Mercy Date. She probably called ten of her cool friends, not to mention her ultraslick boyfriend, Mick Mahoney, to see if anyone else wanted to go. I'm the last resort. And I know that she was probably calling because I have a car, and she doesn't. She just needed a ride. So what would a nondesperate person with at least a shred of pride say? Answer: No.

Good evening, ladies and germs. Meet the Most Desperate Girl in the Universe— Mina Kurtz.

Okay. I can handle not being Miss Popularity at school. Truly. I'm not interested in being yet another mallster who devotes hours to contemplating shoes. But I do miss something that I could only confess here—I miss having a best friend. I miss Camy.

Oops—Camille. Ever since Camy got cool, she decided her nickname was "babyish." And she rolls her eyes every time I use it. For a while, after she dumped me, I liked yelling, "Hey, Camy!" down a crowded hall at school, just to rock her world.

Camille Brentano and I met in second grade, when Camy moved to Mohawk Falls. She was wearing the same color OshKosh overalls as I was, so it was fate. We were inseparable for our whole entire childhoods, and most of high school. We threw mud balls at Jeremy Tulchin together, and we slept over at each other's houses and wore the same jammies as we ate chocolate chip cookies we had baked together.

We even looked a little alike—we both have dark hair and green eyes—except Camy was always a little plump and I was a skinny runt. People thought we were sisters. We both liked that, because neither of us have a sister. I have three older brothers, and Camy was an only child until her father remarried. Then she got two of the worst stepsisters in the world.

In high school, we watched as other girls bought lipstick and went out on dates. We studied and watched TV while other girls went shopping. For our junior prom, we split a pepperoni pizza and Camy made a batch of brownies.

Then Camy went away last summer, before our senior year started. Her mom rented a house at the beach. When she came back, she'd lost fifteen pounds and had a great haircut. She'd even had a summer boyfriend. She didn't look like me anymore.

She had that mysterioso thing called
"style," like she'd stepped out of an MTV
video. Something happened that I call the
"cool jump." She had moved from the nerd
column to the cool column in one huge leap.
She was the star of Mohawk Falls High.
And she was now "Camille" instead of
Camy.

At first, it was totally swell to hear about
her dates, and who called her on the phone,
and all that stuff. But soon, the cool kids
started including her when they went to
hear their favorite bad garage bands, or to
their stupid parties where someone's parents
were out of town and the house got trashed.
And I was most definitely not invited. Not
that I'd go.

I made sure that Camille knew I had the
utmost contempt for that bunch. I practiced
my zingers when I was alone in my room,
and then I'd let them fly and wait for her to
laugh. But after a while, she didn't. So naturally, I just pumped up the volume.

Pretty soon, our friendship hit a dead end
sign head-on at ninety miles an hour.

Then this winter, Camille hooked up with

the coolest guy at school—Mick Mahoney, who is in the loudest and most tuneless of the local bands. That launched her even further into Social Orbit. She even got a tattoo in the shape of a butterfly because he plays in the Dead Butterfly Band. Isn't that just too gag-me sweet?

Camy and I were over, *to use one of the New Camille's favorite words. So when she called me to go malling, I should have laughed and said, "Excuse me, did you dial the right number?" Or I should have sniffed and said, "Like, I have a million major plans that don't include you." Considering what happened after, I definitely should have done anything but what I did.*

But I went.

1//cool jump

"So what store do you want to hit first?" I asked Camille as we walked through the mall entrance.

She shrugged.

Here is an example of one of the things that drives me crazy about the new Camille. It's like any interest or enthusiasm is suddenly uncool. She communicates totally through shrugs, sighs, and eye rolls.

Normally, right about now, I'd make a crack about how Camille might want to test her vocal cords. But I wanted to start out on the right foot. For some totally insane reason, I actually thought we might have a good time that afternoon.

"How about checking out some new CD–ROMs at the computer store?" I asked.

Camille rolled her eyes. She sighed.

"Hey, I know!" I said in a fake cheery voice. "Let's check out the new saucepan display at the Kitchen Korner!"

"Are you totally in-*sane?*" Camille asked.

"I hear they have some new nonstick surfaces," I said. I was goading her. At least I'd gotten her to talk.

She gave a really deep sigh. "Let's check out Riot."

Riot is a store in the mall that sells trendy clothes on the principle that every teenager wants to look like every other teenager. They'll never go broke.

I avoid it on principle, but also because I'd feel stupid wearing what they sell. Call me crazy, but a skintight rubber dress with fluorescent-green racing stripes doesn't make me want to break out into a chorus of "I Feel Pretty." More like, "I Feel Like a Radial Tire."

We flipped through clothes in Riot while alternative rock music thumped in our ears. Camille held up a see–through lace blouse that came with a matching corset. "This is cute," she said.

"Perfect for church!" I approved.

She put it back and flipped lazily through the racks.

I followed behind her. "Isn't it seriously strange how they call it 'alternative rock' when they play it everywhere you go?" I asked.

"Are you going to start?" Camille asked me, her hand on her newly bony hip.

"Start what?" I asked.

"Because if you're going to start, I'm out of here," Camille said.

I wasn't sure what she meant, but I guessed I wasn't supposed to make conversation. So instead, I trailed behind her while she held up various items of clothing, shook them, then slipped them back in the rack. She didn't even bother asking me what I thought.

I held up a short-sleeved sweater I thought was cute.

Camille rolled her eyes. "Bo-ring."

"Actually, I was wondering what kind of boring person would wear this," I said, putting it back. "That's why I picked it up."

"Yeah, right," Camille said.

"Um, Camy?" I said, using her nick-name deliberately. "There's this concept I want to introduce you to? It's called irony. All the smart people are using it. I realize this means that it hasn't reached your crowd."

Camille flipped her long dark hair over her shoulder. "Let's get something to eat," she said.

I shrugged, then nodded. I decided to become an instant freshman in the Camille Brentano Body Language School. As we walked to the food court, I felt a strange sensation, as if a Nerd Fungus was actually growing on my body.

"How about splitting a barbecued chicken pizza?" I suggested.

"I want a Skinni Freeze," Camille said, ignoring my suggestion.

"Yum," I agreed. "Air-injected nondairy chemicals always hit the spot."

Camille gave me a look. I guess it meant, *you're starting*.

So I stopped.

We walked over to the frozen yogurt counter. Camille ordered a vanilla nonfat with strawberries. I said I'd have the same.

The girl just stared at us for a minute. They do not recruit food court employees from M.I.T.

"What flavor did you say?" she asked Camille.

"Vanilla," Camille snapped. "Was my order too complicated for you?"

The girl's face seemed to implode. She was around our age, and had what my mother would call an "unfortunate" complexion. She gazed at Camille, her mouth open.

"With strawberries," I added. I smiled at her so that she wouldn't think both of us were rude.

But she didn't even look at me. She scurried away and hurriedly thrust a plastic dish under the big nozzle. Frozen yogurt began to spiral out in those big droopy logs.

"After this, you want to go kick some puppies?" I asked Camille.

"What's that supposed to mean?" she asked, fishing for her wallet.

"You don't have to treat everyone like

dirt, you know," I said. "You can save it for the people who really deserve it."

Camille's hand stopped moving. Her head was down, and her hair hid her face. I couldn't see her expression.

"Oh," she mumbled. "I've got a lot on my mind today, Mina."

It was the first human thing she'd said all day. We paid the dumpy counter girl and walked to a table in silence.

I dipped a spoon into my yogurt. I let the coolness slide down my throat. Did I dare try to be nice to Camille? Would she just roll her eyes and tell me that concern was lame?

"Want to share it?" I asked.

Camille looked down at her yogurt in confusion. Sometimes, she's not the swiftest.

"Not your yogurt," I said softly. "What's on your mind."

"Oh." Camille picked off a strawberry and ate it. She was wearing baby blue nail polish. "Do you ever chat online, Mina?"

"Not much," I admitted. "Most of the conversations are so stupid. Maybe I can't find the right chat rooms, or something. The ones I click into seem full of every guy you don't want to talk to in your own high school."

"That's true," Camille said. She moved her spoon around in her yogurt, but she didn't take a bite. "But that's in kid chat rooms. There are some cool places to hang out in. Like, for instance, rooms where they just talk about movies."

"I guess that could be cool," I said. But I was imagining a bunch of guys talking about the latest action film and saying, "Awesome, awesome, awesome!"

She dabbed at her mouth with her napkin, even though she hadn't taken a bite yet. "Anyway, I kind of met someone."

"Kind of met?" I asked.

"I met someone, okay?" Camille said. "He's so cool. We've talked for hours and hours. His name is Andrew, and he's a writer."

"Does he write for his school paper?" I asked.

She made a face. "No, he doesn't do kid stuff. He writes screenplays. Actually, he's older."

"How much older?" I asked suspiciously.

"Twenty-four," Camille said, digging up a big spoonful of yogurt.

She put the bite in her mouth and smiled. That's when I knew she was lying.

"How much older?" I repeated.

She swallowed. "Okay. He's twenty-seven."

"Twenty-seven? Camy, are you crazy?" I blurted. "That's way old for you."

"He says I'm really mature for my age," Camille said defensively.

"I'm sure," I said. "What do you think a twenty-seven-year-old man is doing hanging with a seventeen-year-old girl? Do the math, will you? The guy is a pervert!"

"Thanks a lot, Mina." Camille's face was stony. "You really think a lot of my judgment, don't you."

Well, I didn't want to get into that. After all, Camy was dating Mick Mahoney, whose brain had been cloned from Barney Rubble.

"It's not that, Camy," I said.

"Camille!"

"It's that you can't know what somebody's really like when you meet them online."

"I know what Andrew's like," Camille said stubbornly. "He's way more intelligent than any guy I've ever known. He really knows movies and show business. He says he can help me be an actress."

"Right," I said. "I'm sure he's Mr. Hollywood."

"He said that because I won that contest, I could probably get an agent," Camille said.

Last month, Camille had won a Deva Winter look-alike contest. She actually looks a little like the nineteen-year-old actress, who was nominated this year for her first Academy Award. Deva Winter was shooting a movie south of Mohawk Falls down in Saratoga Springs, and the local chapter of the Deva Winter Fan Club had sponsored a contest. Camille had worn a wig, just like Deva's signature hairstyle, and had dressed just like her character in *Sensible Shoes*. She'd won a gift certificate for a Day of Beauty at Shear Heaven, this ultrahip salon.

"Andrew said I should cut my hair like Deva's when I go in for my haircut,"

Camille said. "I can't wait. I'm going next weekend."

"Why should you make yourself into a carbon copy of Deva Winter?" I asked. "That sounds like a stupid idea to me."

Camille ripped a napkin out of the holder and wiped her fingers. "What makes you such a Hollywood expert?"

"I'm not saying I'm an expert," I said carefully. "I'm just saying that Andrew might not be. How do you know he really writes screenplays?"

Camille gave me a cool look. "You know, Mina, I forgot how cynical you are. I remember how it got on my nerves. As soon as I wanted to do something, you always shot it down."

The shaft from Camille's little bow and arrow hit its mark—*ping!* I felt hurt. I slurped some yogurt off my spoon.

"What about Mick?" I asked.

"What about him?" Camille snapped.

"I thought you two were supposed to be the perfect couple," I said. "Why are you cheating on him?"

Camille looked irritated. "I'm not cheating

on him, okay? Just don't worry so much about my personal life."

"I'm not worried," I said, "it's just that—"

"Look, here's the deal." Camille leaned over the table. "Will you come with me when I go to meet him?"

I hesitated, surprised. Why was Camille asking me?

"You're the only one I can trust, Mina."

And I'm the only one who won't blab, I thought, staring into Camille's crystal green eyes. *So it won't get back to Mick.*

But what did the reason matter? Camille was asking me for a favor. The only trouble was, it was a favor I didn't want to grant. I didn't think Camille should meet this guy at all. He sounded bogus. Why was he so interested in a high school kid?

Camille suddenly threw her napkin across the table. "Look, forget it. Just forget it. I should have known better." She stood up, her chair scraping loudly. The yogurt girl looked over at us.

"Calm down," I said to Camille. "I'll go, okay?"

Because if I didn't, Camille might go

alone. And that would be worse.

"As long as it's in a public place," I added.

Camille put her hands on the back of the chair. She leaned toward me, her dark hair swinging. "I'm not going to meet him in his apartment, Mina. I haven't even talked to him on the phone yet. I'm not stupid, no matter what you might think."

"I don't think you're stu—"

"Mina's the smart one," Camille said in a high voice, as though she were mimicking someone. But I had no idea who it was. "If only Camy were quick, like Mina. If only she'd lose that weight."

"Camy—"

"Oh, screw it," Camille said. "You've always been such a wimp, Mina. Toeing the line, being the good girl. Following the rules. You're such a loser!"

"I said I'd go," I protested.

"Like I need you," Camille said. "Like I need anyone." She pulled her purse off the chair. "I'm out of here."

"But I have the car!" I cried, hurrying around the table toward her.

She whipped her big purse over her shoulder, almost slapping me in the face.

"I'll take the bus," she told me, and strode off.

2//serious stuff

So I blew it. So what? It wasn't like Camille and I were still friends. And it wasn't totally my fault. I might have been a teeny bit judgmental. Maybe a little sarcastic. But Camille hadn't exactly been Miss Congeniality. And in the end, she'd ditched me, which is a major teenage no-no. I'd call the whole encounter a draw.

But I still felt guilty.

Camy had always been good at making me feel guilty. She'd made me feel guilty for getting better grades, or for having two parents who stayed together, or for having three brothers to pal around with.

Of course, Mom would say, in her "wise mom" voice, that nobody can make you feel guilty. You do that to yourself. But Mom never had to face Camy's big green eyes fixing on you and saying, *"It's okay, Mina. I don't mind if Mrs. Turkel always gives you A's. I know she thinks you're really smart."*

As if our teacher had decided I was smart because she wanted to, not because I was.

So even today, when I was a lot more grown up, and I knew that Camille had been nasty, I still felt like I should have tried harder. Or at least, I should have kept my wise-guy mouth shut.

I guess I was a tad testy around the house. I yelled at my brother Alex when he hogged the bathroom, even though he had his first date that night with Melinda Vescuso, the girl of his dreams. And I called my brother Douglas "Dermo Doug" because he borrowed my gym shorts and returned them unwashed. It was a scuzzy thing to do, but I shouldn't have made fun of his zits.

About ten o'clock that night, my oldest brother, Matt, who had moved home after college to save money, stuck his head in my doorway. "Will you bite my head off and suck out my eyeballs if I tell you that you have a phone call?" he asked.

"Just let me sharpen my teeth," I said. "Who is it?"

"Mrs. Brentano," he said, heading back down the hall.

I walked slowly to the phone. I couldn't imagine why Mrs. Brentano was calling me. Camille and I were a little old for her mother's "why don't you two make up over some fudgy brownies?" routine.

"Mina, have you seen Camille?" Mrs. Brentano asked me, sounding fluttery and distracted. But Mrs. Brentano always sounds fluttery and distracted. She is a travel agent, and I always picture her clients asking for a cruise to Hawaii and ending up in a Finnish fjord.

"Not since we went to the mall this afternoon," I told her.

"Did you drop her home?" she asked.

"No, we split up there," I said. "Camille said she'd take the bus."

"Oh, dear. That doesn't sound like Camy."

I didn't say anything. I felt sort of embarrassed that Camille and I had had a fight.

"She didn't come home for dinner," Mrs.

Brentano continued. "I mean, I don't think she did. I left a plate in the fridge for her. I was on a date with Jonathan."

Last year, Mrs. Brentano had met Jonathan van Veeder, who is this big-deal type in town. He had once been the mayor, and his family owns about half the town. She'd booked a trip for him after his divorce, and he'd asked her on a date. Maybe she'd given him a great discount. Camille referred to him as Weasel Nose for some reason. "Just what I need," she told me when they got engaged. "Another step-person in my life."

"Maybe she's out with her friends and forgot to leave a note," I told Mrs. Brentano. I wasn't very worried. "Did you try Gigi?"

"Who?"

"Gigi Gigante," I said patiently. Gigi was Camille's new best friend.

"Oh, right. I guess Camy has mentioned her. Do you have her number?"

"No, but let me look it up for you." I reached for the phone book. I flipped through it while Mrs. Brentano babbled in my ear about how moody Camille had been lately, and how she really should give Jonathan a chance. Finally, she wound down and I was able to read her the number.

"Or you can try her boyfriend, Mick," I suggested. "She's probably with him."

"Right," Mrs. Brentano said. "Now, what's his last name again?"

"Mahoney," I said. "I'll look it up."

I looked up Mick's number and suggested a few more kids from that crowd, and then looked them up, too. I told Mrs. Brentano that I was sure Camille would walk through the door any second. She promised to let me know.

Mrs. Brentano called back at eleven-thirty. She didn't even apologize for calling so late.

"No one has seen her, Mina," she said. "Not even that boyfriend. She knows that if she's going to be past eleven, she should call. Even when she's angry at me, she calls. When she gets home, we're going to have a talk. I'm very, very sick and tired of this behavior. I'm not going to get to sleep until after midnight, and Jonathan and I are playing golf early tomorrow."

"Mrs. Brentano, I'm sure she has a good reason," I said lamely.

"Well. Maybe. We'll see. She's punishing me, and that isn't fair, is it, Mina?"

"No, I guess not," I said. "Um, Mrs. Brentano, I guess I'd better get off the phone. I'll call in the morning, okay? Just to make sure Camille got home."

"I'm teeing off at nine," Mrs. Brentano said. "It's at Jonathan's club, Mina!"

"Right," I said. "Okay, then. Good night."

When I was little, Mrs. Brentano was just a mom. She braided Camille's hair, she made macaroni and cheese from a box, she told us to keep it down because she had a splitting headache. I hadn't really thought much about what kind of mom she was until we were teenagers.

That night, as I replaced the phone, I realized that Mrs. Brentano was worried more about missing her golf date than she was about Camille. She was irritated, not worried. She hadn't remembered the name of the girlfriend Camille had been inseparable with for her entire senior year. And she hadn't known Camille's steady boyfriend's last name. My parents would have known my boyfriend's Social Security number. If I had a boyfriend.

And that made me think about why Camille was so hostile and defensive all the time. As I brushed my teeth and got ready for bed, I decided that I'd apologize to Camille tomorrow. I didn't think we were going to be best friends again. But I didn't want to be just another person who let her down.

I slept until nine o'clock the next morning. I hurried into the kitchen and poured a glass of juice.

"It's Sunday," my mom told me sleepily. She was drinking coffee at the table. The remains of an omelette were on her plate, and my dad's plate was in the sink. They usually have Sunday breakfast together, but they've given up on us kids. They content themselves with insisting that the family always have Sunday lunch together after church. We have it at two o'clock, and

Mom and Dad usually cook up a storm. It's the main meal of the day.

"I know," I said, reaching for the phone.

"So why are you rushing?" Mom asked. "And who are you calling?"

"Camille," I said.

She looked at me, surprised. "I haven't heard that name in a while."

Mrs. Brentano answered the phone, so I guessed she hadn't gone to the country club to tee off.

"Hi, Mrs. Brentano, it's Mina. Is Camille home? I mean, is she awake?"

"She's not awake," Mrs. Brentano said. "And she's not home. I can't believe this. I'm really starting to worry."

Starting to worry?

"You mean she never came home last night?" I asked.

Mom looked up, suddenly alert.

"I finally went to sleep," Mrs. Brentano said. "I didn't think I'd sleep a wink, but when I woke up at seven to get ready for my golf game, her bed hadn't been slept in. Do you think I should call the police?"

Mom raised her eyebrows at me, so I

asked Mrs. Brentano to hold on. I covered the mouthpiece and filled Mom in. "She's wondering if she should call the police."

With an exasperated sound, Mom grabbed the receiver. "Elaine, it's Sarah. Of course you should call the police. I'd call them right now. Now, it's just a precaution. I'm sure there's nothing to worry about. Camy probably just slept over at a girlfriend's house and forgot to tell you. Maybe she's upset about something. You know how emotional teenagers are."

Mom made some sympathetic noises into the phone. "Listen, Elaine, why don't I stop over?" she suggested. "It might be easier if you had someone to wait with you." Mom waited a minute. "Well, if it were up to me, I'd call Camy's father. He should know, don't you think?" She looked at her watch. "All right, sweetie. I'll be over in twenty minutes, tops."

Mom hung up the phone. Her gaze met mine. "Do you know anything about this?" she asked me gently. "Is Camy upset about something?"

I shook my head. "No. I mean, she was

kind of bored and cranky yesterday at the mall. But that's standard operating procedure for her."

Mom frowned worriedly. "Why don't you grab some breakfast and come with me? I know Elaine could use the support."

"Sure," I said.

Mom is not really friends with Camille's mother. They know each other because Camy and I had been best friends. But they aren't buddies. It was weird that she'd volunteer to go over there. And that she'd called her sweetie.

Isn't it strange how when grown-ups are worried about something, it makes you feel like things are ten times worse than you'd thought?

Mrs. Brentano opened the door immediately when we knocked. She was dressed in a little yellow skirt, a yellow-and-pink sweater, and her golf shoes. She was even wearing a visor. Her lipstick was perfect, and so was her hair.

When Camille and I had been friends, sometimes I'd been embarrassed when my mother would drop me off and pick me up. Mrs. Brentano always looked perfect, and my mom was usually kind of disheveled. She ran a nursery with my dad, so she usually had dirt under her fingernails, or was wearing a sweatshirt. And she had the kind of short hair that was always messy, no matter what she tried to do with it. But today, I was glad my mother looked messy and distracted. It seemed to fit the circumstances.

"No word," Mrs. Brentano told us. "The police are on their way. Howard had a fit, of course. I told him to stay home, but of course he didn't listen."

Howard is Camy's dad. He and Mrs. Brentano do not get along at all. Mrs. Brentano usually refers to him as "your father" to Camy, in a way that Camy has come to imitate and truly despise.

Thinking about Camy made me even more worried, so when my mom suggested I make a pot of tea, I hightailed it to the kitchen. While I was waiting for the water to boil, the police showed up.

They asked Mrs. Brentano when she'd

last seen Camille, and if Camille had been upset, or if they'd had a fight, or if Camille had boyfriend trouble, or trouble at school. It was pretty obvious that when it comes to her daughter, Mrs. Brentano is clueless.

Then Mr. Brentano burst in with his wife. He started shouting at Mrs. Brentano about not calling him the night before. He seemed more angry about her lack of "parental respect" than the fact that Camille was missing. Then he finally noticed the cops. So he got all teary about his daughter, and his wife had to fetch him a glass of water. It really was enough to make you sick.

Then the police interviewed me. Both of them were overweight, one of them with skinny legs and a big paunch. The other was big all over, and his hair looked like it was slipping off the back of his head, like a blanket falling off your bed on a cold night. I told them that we had shopped together, had a yogurt, and then Camille had decided to take the bus back home from the mall. They wrote things down, and I tried to peek at them, but I couldn't see anything.

"Why did Camille take the bus home, if you had a car?" the cop with the sliding hair asked.

"She wanted to shop more," I said, shrugging. "Or she was sick of me, I guess. We're not very good friends anymore."

His gaze lingered on me for a minute. I forced myself to sit still and not squirm. Maybe I should have told them about the argument, but I just felt too guilty. And I knew it hadn't been important enough to make Camille run away.

The doorbell rang, and Mrs. Brentano gasped, which is funny, because if it had been Camille, she'd have used her key. Camille's stepmother, Darcy, opened the door. Mick Mahoney blinked at the sight of a room full of strangers in Camille's living room.

"The boyfriend," the cop said softly.

"Is she still missing?" Mick asked. He ran a hand through his hair, which was thick and straight and the color of wheat. His black leather motorcycle jacket was a little big for him, and the cuffs grazed his knuckles.

"Not a word," Mrs. Brentano said.

"Oh," Mick said. I told you how brilliant he was.

The cop turned back to me. "Was there anything else?" he asked.

"Well, I don't know if it's important or not," I said. "Camille had met this guy online, and she wanted me to go with her to meet him sometime. I said that sounded totally crazy, but I finally said I'd do it. But it's not like we made a definite plan."

Both cops perked up. They exchanged looks. "Another boyfriend?"

I looked over at Mick. He seemed surprised, but when he caught me looking, he studied Mrs. Brentano's curtains.

"Sort of," I said. "He's older—twenty-seven, I think. They'd been chatting for a couple of weeks, I guess. But she said she wouldn't meet him alone."

"Older?" Mrs. Brentano asked. "Camille didn't tell me about this."

The doorbell rang again. This time it was Mrs. Brentano's fiancé, Jonathan van Veeder. He was dressed in a green golfing sweater, green plaid pants, and white shoes. If Camille had been here, there would have been some major eye-rolling activity going on.

"Oh, Jonathan!" Mrs. Brentano ran to him. They exchanged a big golf hug. "She's not back yet. The police are here."

One of the policemen turned back to me. "Did she say where this guy lives, or what his name is?" he asked me quietly.

I bit my lip, trying to remember. "Andrew!" I said, relieved. "His name is Andrew. But I don't know his last name, or where he lives."

"You're doing fine," the cop said.

They asked me a few more questions, then said they'd have to get someone over to search Camille's computer and her hard drive. They told Mrs. Brentano that Camille would probably show up on her own, but they were going to go all out to find her.

Mrs. Brentano started to cry. "My baby ran away," she said. She hid her head in Jonathan van Veeder's sweater. "Please find her," she said in a muffled voice.

"I want you to do everything, do you understand?" Mr. Brentano said to the police hoarsely.

Mom told Mrs. Brentano that she'd call her that evening. Everyone filed out. Mick got into his beatup Volkswagen Bug, and Mom and I slid into our car.

"What a freak show," I said disgustedly as Mom drove slowly home. "Mrs. Brentano is mostly ticked because she didn't get to bat a golf ball around. Mr. Brentano is using Camille to get back at his ex. And they both put on this big show for the cops."

Mom sighed as she coasted to a stop. "Mina, the Brentanos might not be the best parents in the world. But they aren't the worst. It's never a good idea to judge people. Especially under these circumstances."

"I can't help it," I said. "I judge people all the time. It's my favorite form of entertainment."

I was trying to joke, but Mom didn't smile. She just patted my hand on the seat. "I know, sweetie," she said sadly.

She drummed her fingers on the steering wheel. "Poor Elaine," she said.

Mom hit the gas, and we took off for home. We'd be late for Sunday lunch. Dad had told us before we left that he was making roast chicken. He always stuffs garlic under the skin and rubs it with lemons. My stomach rumbled just thinking about how delicious it was. Then I felt guilty. What was Camille eating?

As if Mom had had the same thought, she asked suddenly, "Do you think Camy ran away, Mina?"

I thought about it. I remembered how Camille had been looking forward to cashing in that gift certificate at the salon. She'd talked about the new haircut she was planning to get. Sure, she'd been cranky that day. But she hadn't seemed really depressed, or more bored or restless than usual. And I sure didn't think that a fight with me would send her packing.

"No," I said. "I don't think she did, somehow."

"Did anything happen at the mall that you're not telling me?" Mom asked.

"Of course not," I said.

"It just seems funny that Camy would take the bus," Mom went on.

"She was tired of my company," I said. "She's way past cool, and I'm a resident of zeroville."

"Mina, I wish you'd stop talking that way," Mom said, pulling into the driveway. "You're a lovely, smart girl, and you're just as pretty as Camille."

"Mom, you're such a mom," I said.

She turned off the ignition and turned to me. "Would you really have gone with Camille to meet this strange man, this Andrew?"

"Of course not," I said. It wasn't a lie, because I wasn't sure I would have gone. Knowing me, I would have knuckled under, just to please Camy. Just hoping she'd be my friend again. "I just said yes because I didn't want her to make a big deal."

"Do you think she would have gone alone?" Mom asked.

"No," I said, shaking my head. "Definitely not. It was the way she said she wouldn't. I knew she wasn't lying."

Mom sighed. "We just have to hope for the best. I'm sure Camy will show up today."

"And be grounded for the next six months," I said.

"Let's hope so," Mom said. Then she leaned over and hugged me. She hung on for an extra moment, and I let her. After all, she is a mom.

"Poor Elaine," she said again.

Poor Camille, I thought, but I didn't have to say it. I knew Mom was thinking it, too.

3//come home, camille

Camille didn't show up that day, or the next. The bus drivers didn't remember her boarding the bus to leave the mall. Camille is a knockout, and so they all said they'd most likely remember her, as it was a slow day.

The police read all her e-mail, and even cleaned out her hard drive in case she'd erased a letter saying where she was planning to meet Andrew. But they didn't find anything.

Since it was spring break, I didn't have school, and time felt like a piece of Silly Putty that was being str-et-ch-ed to the limit. I tried to read, I rented videos, I called up friends. But all we ever talked about was Camille's disappearance, and that's all I ever thought about, too.

Mom called Mrs. Brentano each day. There was never any news, and she always said the same thing: that Camille is a bright, resourceful girl who can take care of herself. Mrs. Brentano was convinced that Camille had headed for L.A. or New York City to find work as an actress.

Monday night I asked Mrs. Brentano if I could read Camille's e-mail exchange with Andrew, just in case I could come up with clues that the police had missed. She handed over a stack of paper, and I took it home to go through it.

If part of me had been hoping that I would have a flash of intuition and astonish everyone with my brilliance, all of me was disappointed. I was just as clueless as the cops. Camille and Andrew had chatted about movies, her desire to be an actress, and the fact that she looks like Deva Winter. Andrew had even been at the look-alike contest, but they hadn't spoken, and Camille hadn't remembered him. The only thing of interest I did discover was Andrew's last name, Sloane.

The funny thing is that their exchange wasn't like a flirtation, really. It was more like friends. I wondered if Camille was putting more into the exchange than this guy Andrew had.

I asked Mrs. Brentano if the police had investigated Andrew's e-mail address, 2ofhearts, but whoever it was had closed their account. They were still trying to track down his address.

Jonathan van Veeder's brother, Charles, owns the local television station, and one night, Mr. and Mrs. Brentano went on the local news. My whole family gathered around the set to watch it.

A picture of Camille flashed onscreen. I'd never seen it before, but I guessed it was taken last summer, at the beach. Camille was smiling, and her hair was blowing back from her face. She was wearing a white T-shirt and blue jeans. She looked fantastic.

"This is our daughter, Camille," Mr. Brentano said. "We miss her so much. Camille, if you're out there, we need to talk to you, honey. Please come home."

"If something upset you, we'll fix it,"
Mrs. Brentano said. "And if you're with
someone . . . if someone took you away,
please, just call." Mrs. Brentano started to
cry. "I miss you so much. Come home,
Camille."

The segment ended, and we all just sat
there, staring. Isn't it seriously strange how
TV can make something suddenly seem so
real, when TV is so fake?

I was going crazy sitting around the
house, so the next morning, I headed to
school. It was closed, but I figured somebody would be around to let me in. Sure
enough, Mr. Mataleno, the head of main-
tenance, was doing some sort of mainte-
nance thing and answered my knock. I
told him I needed something out of my
locker, and he scowled and told me to
hurry it up, pronto. Mr. Mataleno
always scowls and tells you to hurry it
up, pronto.

But I didn't head for my locker. I headed
for Camille's. We'd known each other's
locker combinations since freshman year,

and I was hoping she hadn't changed the lock.

She hadn't. I didn't know what I was looking for, but I figured she wouldn't mind if I poked around. I didn't know if the police had gone through her stuff, but they probably didn't know what to look for, either.

Books, cassette tapes for her Walkman, a denim jacket. A pair of orange high-tops. A balled-up pair of socks.

I sat down on the floor and drew a pile of books on my lap. I began to rifle through them. Maybe I'd find a note from Andrew. When I got to her loose-leaf binder, I flipped through it. There were notes from her classes, but there were mostly doodles. Every so often a note to herself would be highlighted, like **tell Gigi about SALE** and **crystal earrings ! ! !** and once, **tube socks—bogus or radical? ? ?**

Camille isn't the best student. It seems like she spends most of her time in class thinking about her wardrobe. In the beginning of the notebook were drawings of Mick's initials that had been shaded and elongated, then built into bridges and hearts and buildings. There was also a concentration on butterfly drawings. But the Mick phase seemed to end, and there were once again drawings of shoes and boxes and clocks, just aimless doodles to pass the time.

"Find anything?"

I turned. Mick Mahoney was standing at the end of the hall. He was dressed in a striped T-shirt and ripped jeans that made him look like a twelve-year-old kid on a playground who had just fallen off the slide.

"No," I said, closing the notebook. "What are you doing here?"

He leaned against a locker. "Same thing you are, I guess. I thought maybe there'd be a clue or something in Camille's locker. Why she ran away."

"She didn't run away," I blurted.

Mick straightened. "Did her parents get a ransom note?" he asked. His face went tense, and he didn't look like a little kid anymore.

"No," I said quickly. "There's been no word at all. It's just a feeling I have, that's all." I started to replace the books in her locker. "I'd better clear out. I told Mr. Mataleno that I'd—"

"Hurry it up, pronto," Mick finished.

We grinned at each other, and I felt a tiny bit more comfortable with him.

Mick squatted down a few inches from me. "You two were pretty tight until this year, right?"

"Yeah," I said.

"So what happened?"

"Life happened," I said, tossing the books back in the locker. I was suddenly angry at him. He knew what had happened. All he had to do was look at me and look at Camille. Obviously, she'd suddenly vaulted to superstar status.

"But you still probably know her better than Gigi Gigante does," Mick said in his soft voice. He never raised his voice, even when I was banging books in a locker. "Gigi is a pond skimmer."

"A what?"

Mick held out his hand and moved it, fluttering his fingers. "She skims the surface."

"And what makes you think I'm a person of such great depth?" I asked sarcastically. "I resent that. I'm as superficial as the next guy, fella."

"I read your column," he said.

Oh. I write a stupid column for the high school paper, called "Rants." In it, I basically complain about everything I hate about high school. I didn't think anybody read it, except people like me who look at high school from the bleachers.

Mick lowered himself to the floor. He leaned against a locker and stretched out one long leg. "So if you don't think she ran away, that means you think she was kidnapped."

"I didn't say that," I snapped. I didn't even want to think that Camille had been snatched by some sicko. But it was what I'd been thinking all along. "Okay, I'm thinking it," I added grudgingly. "But I don't want to."

"Do the police still think she took off?"

"There was this report of some girl hitchhiking on the Taconic Parkway. So they're checking it out. Plus, there hasn't been a ransom note. And why the Brentanos? They don't have big bucks."

"But Jonathan van Veeder does," Mick said.

"I'm sure the police are aware of that," I said.

"So if you were the police," Mick said, "what would you do?"

I shrugged. "I don't know. Trace her last movements. Interview her friends. Pass around her picture. I guess they're doing all that."

"Why don't we do it?" Mick asked.

I looked at him. "Do what?"

"Investigate," he said. "It beats sitting around and worrying, doesn't it? Maybe we could turn up something the cops didn't. We know Camille, and they don't."

I wanted to say no. Mostly because Mick had thought of the idea, not me. But he was right—I would go crazy if I just continued to sit around and wait.

"I guess we could poke around," I said. "Tell me, Columbo. Where should we start?"

"At where she was last seen, of course.

That's where the police always start. Don't you ever watch TV?"

"I'm way too profound," I said.

"Listen, I don't say this often in life," Mick said. "But do you want to go to the mall?"

4//last seen wearing

I stopped home to get a picture of Camille and to drop off my car. I left a note telling Mom who I was with and where I was. She'd gotten extra vigilant lately about that stuff. I didn't blame her. Until Camy was found, I wanted someone to know where I was at all times. Now there's a behavioral change for you.

Mick and I checked every shop that Camille might have visited after she left me, and even ones she'd never visit in a million years, like the Learning Curve, which is filled with educational books and games, and On the Road, which sells maps and stupid things for your car like compasses and CBs.

The salesgirl at Riot remembered Camille, but Camille is a regular there. And the girl at the Pure & Natural, a cosmetics store, remembered her, too. But both of them couldn't remember if Camille had been there last Saturday, or the Saturday before, or even what time they'd seen her. They just remembered her face. Everyone always remembers Camille's face.

It was tiring, not to mention boring, to have to go to each store. But we kept on until we'd covered the entire first floor. We ended up at the food court.

"I'm an idiot," I said suddenly. "We should talk to the girl at the yogurt counter. Maybe Camille came back to talk to me again, apologize or something—"

"Apologize for what?" Mick asked.

I shrugged. "I don't know. Ditching me."

"Camille never apologizes," Mick said.

I was about to defend her, but then I realized he was right. "Or maybe she changed her mind and wanted a ride home."

"That sounds more like Camille," Mick said. "Come on."

But a different girl was at the counter when we came by. I described the other server, and she nodded before I'd gotten much past "Dark hair, kind of stocky, and she had a teeny break-out problem—"

"Katie," she interrupted. "Definitely. Let me look up her next shift for you." She consulted a sheet of paper tacked up near the register. "Thursday night. The shift starts at four-thirty and ends at nine-thirty, when the mall closes."

We thanked her and turned away.

"So maybe we should stop back here on Thursday," I said to Mick.

He nodded. "Let's hit the second floor now. Then afterward, maybe we can go back to your place and we can do some brainstorming."

I was irritated. It sounded like an order.

"Okay," I said grumpily. "Let's get this over with. If I stay too long at the mall, I start to get hives."

"I get them in the parking lot," Mick said.

Back at my house, I showed Mick the e-mail, but he didn't discover any clues, either. And reading letters she wrote to another guy didn't seem to bother him, even though in her last e-mail Camille had told Andrew *most of the guys I know are complete wimps.*

"Doesn't it bug you to read these?" I prodded.

Mick was frowning over the letters. "Hmmm? No, not really." He tapped one of the letters and looked up at me. "Look, Mina," he said. "He met her at that lame Deva Winter look-alike contest. He says he saw her receive the prize."

"But Camille didn't see *him,*" I said. "So she didn't see what he looks like."

"But maybe someone else did," Mick said. "It wasn't a huge contest. And let's face it, how many people go to see a Deva Winter look-alike contest at some stupid restaurant?"

"Fried clams were only $5.99," I said. "You never know."

He raised a corner of his mouth, as though committing to a full grin would tire him out too much. "Do you know who organized the contest?"

"It was the local chapter of the Deva Winter Fan Club," I said.

"Maybe this is one way to trace this guy," Mick said. "Look, I might as well say what we're both thinking. Sure, Camille said she wouldn't meet him alone. But what if he was at the mall that day? What if he charmed her? What if he offered her a ride home? Isn't that what you're thinking?"

I nodded slowly. "It's occurred to me, yeah."

"Well, if he kidnapped Camille, that's where he met her. Let's find out some more about that contest."

"Let's make some calls," I said.

5//number one fans

The contest had been sponsored by the Northeast Chapter of the Deva Winter Fan Club. The club's headquarters was in Albany. I called the president, Ronnie Harbin, and asked if we could talk to her in person.

"I work, you know," she said impatiently. Not the friendliest of individuals.

"It wouldn't take long," I said. "We just need to ask you a couple things." Then, I had an inspiration. "We could take you to lunch."

"Lunch" must have been the magic word. "I guess so," she said. "I'm wearing peach today."

So Mick and I drove down to Albany in his rattletrap Bug. The rear window didn't close completely, and the combination of cool wind and clattering noise made me feel as though I were riding inside an ancient air conditioner that had been stuck in a window and left to die.

"There's this theory about guys and their cars," I said. "Something about how a guy chooses a car because it turns a drawback he has into an advantage. For example, fat guys choose big, huge Cadillacs to make themselves look skinny."

I was totally making all of this up. But I considered it my mission in life just now to annoy Mick Mahoney. He needed to know that not every girl at Mohawk High thought he was serious hot stuff.

"Mmm," Mick said. He was concentrating on keeping the tiny car on the road. Every time a gust of wind hit, we almost turned into Dorothy inside the tornado in *The Wizard of Oz*.

"So someone who chooses a Volkswagen Bug probably thinks he's too short," I went on. I'd already noted that Mick was only about an inch and a half taller than I was and I'm only five five. "In his mind, he thinks he'll look tall getting out of it. So he'll search high and low for the smallest car he can, even if it's practically falling apart. He'd be that desperate to look tall and powerful. I mean, if you believe in the theory, that is."

There was a moment of silence. The wind whistled through the broken window.

"So how tall are you, Mick?" I asked innocently.

"Taller than you," he growled.

He gave me a sidelong look out of his famous (at least among the girls of Mohawk High) golden brown eyes. I smiled cheerfully at him.

"You know, being nice to me is always an option," he said.

"I'll consider it," I said.

I could see that I'd steamed him a little. so I relaxed and enjoyed the rest of the ride.

When we got to Albany, we followed Ronnie's directions and parked at a lot near her office. She works in some sort of government building, and we waited outside on the steps. Right on time, a tall, plump young woman in dangerously high pumps walked out and stood at the top of the steps. She was probably about nineteen, but it was obvious she was attempting a dress-for-success look. She wore a peach suit that was a little too tight. The jacket buttons pulled a bit, revealing the striped shirt she wore beneath. She checked us out nervously.

"Ronnie Harbin?" I said. When she nodded, I said, "I'm Mina Kurtz, and this is Mick Mahoney. Thanks for meeting us."

"S'okay," she said. She looked a little wary. Maybe it was Mick's motorcycle jacket, or his long hair.

Mick gave her the full effect of his heart-stopping (according to Mohawk High senior girls) grin. "It's a beautiful day, isn't it?" he said. He took a step toward her and stopped. His voice lowered. "Please don't hate me for saying this. But you remind me so much of my cousin Hassie. I had such a major crush on her when I was six. At seven, she broke my heart."

I waited for Ronnie to roll her eyes and say, *tell me another one, buster*. But, instead, she actually blushed. She ducked her head and smiled at Mick.

"Oh, brother," I muttered. Mick stepped on my foot.

"Where's your favorite place to eat lunch, Ronnie?" Mick asked. "Because that's where we want to take you."

And he actually crooked his arm, like some English lord in a movie. She slipped her arm into it, and they walked off. I trailed behind like a lady-in-waiting, my usual role in life. And I hated Mick Mahoney, at that moment, for forcing me into it.

Ronnie turned out to like her food. A club sandwich with extra bacon ("Oh, go ahead and have it," Mick said. "Girls worry too much about their weight.") and a chocolate shake cheered her right up.

"It's an exciting time for the club," Ronnie said, offering her French fries to Mick. "Deva is right here in our own backyard. I never dreamed such a thing would happen."

"What makes you such a big fan of Deva's, Ronnie?" Mick asked.

"Well, it isn't for the usual things," Ronnie said. "I mean, she's a major beauty, right? And a fabulous actress. But I first starting liking her when I read about her childhood. It was really lonely. She didn't have a father. She never even met him—he left her mom when she was two." Ronnie's hand stilled, and she dropped her French fry. "I know what that's like."

"I do, too, Ronnie," Mick told her in this totally sincere voice. "It's tough."

She nodded and lost herself in Mick's gaze. Her big brown eyes were like chocolates slowly melting in the sun. I was about to lose my lunch. What a con man!

Ronnie shook herself like a bird. She dabbed her mouth with her napkin and cleared her throat. "Anyway, I thought, this girl is just like me."

Yeah, right, I thought. *Ronnie Harbin— Deva Winter. I get them confused all the time.*

"And everything I read about her, I really liked," Ronnie said. "She's the kind of girl who you wish was your friend."

"Do you think you'll get to meet her while she's here?" Mick asked. He took a bite of his grilled-cheese sandwich.

"Oh, I hope so," Ronnie breathed. "I've

written to her publicist and everything, and he promised to ask her. Deva is totally devoted to her fans. We were really hoping that she'd show up at that look-alike contest."

"Which brings us to the point of why we wanted to meet you, Ronnie," I said firmly. I was tired of watching Mick Mahoney flirt his way through the meal.

Ronnie tore her gaze away from Mick. "Oh, right. Something about a friend of yours?"

"Camille," I said. "She won the contest."

"I remember her really well," Ronnie said, in a way that told me that Camille had not been her sweetest self on that day. She would probably take one look at Ronnie and think *loser*.

"She's missing," I said. "The cops don't know whether she ran away or has been kidnapped. She's Mick's girlfriend," I added.

I hoped that would dampen Ronnie's ardor, but instead, it made her melt further. A soft "oh" escaped her, and she covered Mick's hand with hers. Her fingernails matched her suit, but her polish was chipped. She must have noticed, because she quickly pulled her hand away.

"I'm so, so sorry," she breathed. "How awful."

"Thanks," Mick said. "It's really hard on Camille's parents."

"I'm sure."

"So we were wondering, Ronnie, if you saw anyone unusual at the contest. Someone who was staring at Camille, for example," Mick said.

"Think hard," I said. "Go over the day in your mind."

"Well, I got there early because I wanted to make sure everything was perfect," Ronnie said, looking at Mick. He gave her an approving nod. "I was really hoping that Deva would show up. I wore my favorite suit—not this one. It's blue."

I wanted to interrupt and speed Ronnie along, but Mick gave me a warning look.

"All the contestants showed up. Camille was wearing a wig, I remember—just like that new waif cut that Deva got. Do you know that haircut is the most requested one in hair salons around the country?" Ronnie asked. "Anyways, let me think. There was a crowd, but the restaurant was offering this great fried clam special, and honestly, I think more people came for that."

I gave Mick a triumphant look.

"So it was kind of crowded. No, I don't remember seeing anyone unusual, or anyone who stared at the contestants or anything."

"Are you sure?" Mick asked. "Close your eyes."

Ronnie obediently closed her eyes and frowned.

"Does the name Andrew Sloane mean anything?" I asked.

Ronnie's frown deepened, but just then, the waitress came up and cleared away our plates. "Dessert?"

Ronnie hesitated.

"Oh, go on," Mick urged. "Let's all split something."

"Well," Ronnie said, "they have the best banana cream pie."

"We'll take two," Mick told the waitress.

"I really don't remember anything unusual," Ronnie told us. "And I think I would have noticed someone creepy. I was being extra careful, considering."

"Considering what?" I asked.

The waitress slid two pieces of pie the size of sofa cushions onto the table. She pushed three forks toward us.

Ronnie dug in. "Considering the stalker," she said. "I mean, I was thinking that Deva might show up. If something had happened, I would have *died*."

Mick and I exchanged glances. "Stalker?" I asked. I picked up my fork, but I didn't take any pie.

"Poor Deva." Ronnie sighed, forking up another bite of pie. "She had this stalker in L.A. She had to get a restraining order. So you see why I was being extra careful at the contest."

Suddenly, I had an inspiration. "Did you take pictures?"

Ronnie nodded. "Of course."

"Do you think you could send us copies?" I asked. "I'll pay for them."

"That's okay," Ronnie said. "I always get two copies of my prints. I'll just send them." She beamed at Mick.

Ronnie and Mick devoured the two slices of pie, and I watched Ronnie send him moony glances over the whipped cream. Luckily, she had a "very strict lunch hour— my boss is like, this major jerk," so we had to leave. Mick and I split the bill, and we walked her back.

We both shook Ronnie's hand when we said good-bye, but she clung to Mick's for about ten minutes, saying how neat it was to meet him. She parted from him without a tear, thank goodness. She did, however, walk into the brass rail on her way to the door of the building.

"Well, at least we'll get the pictures," Mick said on our way back to the parking lot.

I didn't say anything.

"So the afternoon wasn't a total waste," he added.

"No, it wasn't a total waste," I said. "I got to see Mick Mahoney in action. Don't you think it was mean to flirt with Ronnie? All that stuff about her reminding you of your cousin Hassie! I bet you don't even have a cousin. What kind of a name is

Hassie, anyway? Where are you from, Green Acres?"

"I do have a cousin Hassie," Mick said mildly. "Ronnie didn't really remind me of her, though. But I could tell she was nervous about going off with me."

"It was mean," I said. "You made her feel pretty."

Mick looked puzzled. "That's mean?"

"She's not!" I exclaimed.

"Yes, she is," Mick said. "She has big brown eyes and a great smile."

"She's overweight," I said. "You wouldn't ask her for a date in a million years. And you played along with her, telling her to order all that food so you could laugh at her. And you had the nerve to say that girls worry too much about their weight."

"Girls *do* worry too much about their weight," Mick said. "I was just trying to be nice to her," he said. "You might want to think about working on your people skills. You treated her like a tissue you just blew your nose in."

"Are you through?" I asked, annoyed.

"No," he said, stopping beside his car.

"Stop making fun of my car. I slaved for months to pay for it. And it's the best I can afford."

We got into the car. Mick shifted into first and took off with a jerk.

And maybe the jerk was me.

Ronnie must have mailed the pictures immediately, because I got them the following day. She'd enclosed a note, and I ran to the phone to call Mick to read it to him.

"She remembered where she heard the name Andrew Sloane," I told him excitedly. "I guess she got distracted by the banana cream pie. But it's the name of a character in the Deva Winter movie *Two of Hearts*."

"Which is his e-mail address," Mick said. "How dumb could we be? So Andrew Sloane is definitely an alias. We'd better tell the police."

"The FBI is involved now, too," I told him. "It's being treated as a possible kidnapping."

"I'll see you in ten minutes," Mick said.

I looked down at my pajamas. "Huh?"

"We've got to look at those pictures

before we turn them over," Mick said. "And there's no time to lose."

Mick was over in nine minutes. I just had time to slip on jeans and a T-shirt and bundle my hair back into a ponytail. I spread the pictures out on the dining room table, and we went through them.

"I don't see anyone suspicious," I said. "Not that a kidnapper would look suspicious. It's not like he'd be wearing a big black hat."

Mick stared at a picture of Camille. It had been taken just after she'd won. She looked different in the short wig she'd worn for the contest. Older, more mature. But still gorgeous. She was smiling, and her eyes were alight.

"I hope she's all right," Mick said. He touched Camille's face lightly with a fingertip.

It was the first time I'd caught a glimpse of how much Mick must have loved Camille. I almost felt like Ronnie Harbin. I felt like covering Mick's hand with mine and saying, *oh, how terrible for you*. But I didn't.

I looked back down at the pictures. And

suddenly, a face in the crowd made sense. "Mick!" I exclaimed. I stabbed at a face in the crowd. "I know this girl. She's the girl at the yogurt counter!"

"Are you sure?" he asked.

"I'm sure," I said, staring at it. "What was her name again? Katie? Maybe she saw something that day."

"It's another reason to talk to her, anyway," Mick said.

"And maybe we shouldn't wait until Thursday night," I said.

Mick nodded. "Let's head for the mall."

"I'm sorry," the girl behind the counter said. She shook her short blond curls. "I'm not allowed to give out addresses of employees. That's like, so totally against the rules."

I slumped against the counter. Dead end.

Mick leaned across the counter. Suddenly, he seemed shy. His smile was tentative. "Please don't hate me for saying this. But you remind me so much of my cousin Hassie. . . ."

6//close, so close

From the electronic diary of BIGFAN#1

At first, she wasn't even scared, which was better. It was more like we were friends. Then when she saw where we were going, she got kind of nervous. She told me to let her go, said she'd scream and all that. But now, everything is okay. Everything is fine. She's quiet. She knows that I only want to be with her. She keeps complaining about a headache, because of that lump on her head, but I don't have aspirin, and I don't want to leave yet. I have food and water. She'll get better. She's really strong. She works out every day, and she has nutritionists and personal trainers and everything.

Wait. That's Deva. This is Camille. I really have to work to keep them straight.

But Camille really really looks like Deva. Especially now that I cut her hair like Deva's. She got so scared when I came in with the scissors. She almost got loose from the ropes! I should have studied some kind of rope-tying manual, I guess. Maybe I should buy one. But the cut she got on her forehead was really all her fault. I didn't mean to do it.

She looks so pretty now. Like Deva. I showed her in the mirror. I got so mad, though. When she wouldn't stop crying. I started yelling, "Look what I did! You're beautiful now! Look!" and she just kept crying crying crying. So annoying! I wanted to smash the mirror. I wanted to cut her. With the pieces. But then she stopped crying, so I didn't have to.

Now she knows I made her beautiful. She said so. I know we're starting to be friends. She needs a best friend. She said so. But all the magazines say that friendship takes time. That's okay. We have all the time in the world.

7//the prettiest little girl in the world

"You're disgusting," I told Mick in the car. "I'm starting to like you, too," he said. He grinned as he shifted into second.

"Does that stuff actually work on girls?" I asked. I crossed my arms and stared out the window. "It makes me ashamed of my own sex."

"You don't understand, Mina," Mick said. "All pretty girls do remind me of my cousin Hassie. It's this deep, profound connection that sends me back to my childhood. It could be connected to some major trauma that I've completely blocked. I probably need therapy." Mick gave a theatrical sigh.

"Tell me something I don't know," I said.

We bickered all the way to the neighboring town of Garth, where Katie lives. Then we got lost, and I told Mick he had no sense of direction. He told me I didn't know how to read a map. By the time we reached the tiny frame house, we were ready to trade punches.

We sat in the car, staring at the house. Garth is one of those Upstate New York towns that modern life has passed by. It was settled when the railroad still ran through, so the houses were big and substantial, with porches and fireplaces and turrets. Once, people took the train to Albany, or they worked in the factories in towns like Mohawk Falls, which are on the river. But now there's no industry here, and no way out. Nothing to do, and plenty of time. The houses aren't so grand now. The porches sag, and the paint is peeling.

Katie lived on a street of small, modest homes. But while most of the houses look shabby, this one tried to look snappy. The exterior hadn't been painted in a while, but the windowsills on the first floor were painted bright pink. A lawn ornament that looked like a blue metallic bowling ball sat on a curved concrete base. Near the front porch, some straggly daffodils were trying to poke up through the dirt.

We got out and rang the bell. A series of tones rang out in a melody I didn't recognize. A moment later, the door swung open.

A woman peered at us through the screen in a friendly way. She had permed blond hair that cascaded down her back in a high ponytail. She was thin, and wearing turquoise jeans with a matching cotton sweater. She couldn't have been related to Katie. I remembered the girl as stocky and dark.

"Hiya. Can I help you?" she asked.

"Hi," I said. "Is Katie home? We wanted to talk to her."

The woman frowned. "Katie? She's not here."

"We're friends of hers," Mick said. "Will she be back soon?"

She looked at me, then Mick. "You're not friends of Katie's," she said, her eyes shrewd.

Oops. "Well, we're not *friends*," I said, shooting a warning look at Mick. "But we know her from the mall, where she works."

"The mall?" The woman looked blank. "Katie . . . works at the mall?"

"At the Skinni Freeze," I said. "The frozen yogurt place?"

The woman fluffed her bangs. She frowned. She let out a breath. Then she opened the screen door. "Maybe you'd better come in," she said.

We followed her down a short hallway and turned right. The living room was done entirely in shades of pale green, with dark blue pillows. It sounds awful, but it actually wasn't bad. It would look cool and inviting on a hot day.

"I'm an interior decorator," the woman said, watching my face. "Do you like it? It was an experiment."

"I do like it," I said. "I feel like I'm inside a big plant."

She laughed. "Well, I was thinking more like a garden, but thanks. Everything is slip-covered for spring. I sew them myself. In the winter, I like to use warm tones. I have this whole idea about changing your living room for each season. I'm trying to market my designs, but it's tough."

She motioned to the sofa. "You guys sit. Do you want some soda?"

"No, thanks," we said together.

"I'm Chrissie Farmer," the woman said. "Katie's mother." She lit a cigarette, then waved it at us. "Okay if I smoke?"

That was pretty polite, considering we were in her house. "Sure," I said, and Mick nodded.

She blew out a plume of smoke. "Kids today are so strict. Not like my generation. I should tell you guys that I haven't seen Katie in two years. She ran away. Are you sure we're talking about the same girl?"

"She gave this as her home address," Mick said.

The cigarette stopped halfway to Chrissie's lips. "She did? Wow. I wonder if that means she's going to come home!"

"So you haven't seen her?" I asked.

She sighed. "You probably think I'm a terrible mother."

Mick and I shook our heads fervently. "No, of course not," Mick said.

"She probably told you stories, right?" Chrissie blew out smoke. She crossed her legs. She was wearing metallic gold loafers and she swung one foot nervously back and forth.

I squeezed Mick's hand so that he wouldn't say anything. I had a feeling that if we kept our mouths shut, Chrissie would talk. At this point, I didn't know why we were there, or how she could help us. But maybe she'd let something slip that would give us a lead on Katie.

"Katie wanted to enter the contests," she said. "I never pushed her. She used to love it."

"Contests?" I prompted.

Chrissie went to a sideboard unit and opened a cabinet door. Leather-bound albums lined three shelves. The initials K.D.P. were engraved on each one.

"Scrapbooks and photos," she said, choosing one. She ran a hand over the leather. Then she came back and sat down between us on the pale green sofa, making us scoot away to give her room.

"Do you want to see?" she asked eagerly.

Over Chrissie's permed curls, Mick met my gaze. He jerked his head toward the door, meaning, *let's get out of here!*

But Chrissie was already starting to turn the pages. And I felt sorry for her. She seemed lonesome, here in her coordinated living room, in her coordinated outfit, and in her carefully styled hair. She had lost her daughter, just like Camille's mom. That didn't mean there was a connection, but it did mean we might owe her a little bit of time.

"We'd love to see the photos," I said, ignoring Mick.

Chrissie pointed to a large, glossy photo. A young child—maybe three or four—was smiling at the camera, her head tilted slightly to one side. She was wearing pink lipstick, and she was dressed in a pink satin dress with white cowboy boots. She was blond and fine-boned and looked nothing like the girl I remembered from the mall. But then I recognized the big dark eyes.

"You see how pretty she was?" Chrissie ran a hand over the photo. "The prettiest little girl in the world. This was taken when she won Little Miss Farm Machinery."

Mick coughed and cleared his throat. It sounded like he was trying to smother a laugh.

"And what's this one?" I asked quickly, pointing to another photo. This time, Katie was dressed in a long gown and a feather boa. Her hair was piled on top of her head.

"That was the Little Miss Princess of Hudson Valley," Chrissie said. "And she won Prettiest Smile that time, too. Her talent was dancing to 'You Must Have Been a Beautiful Baby.' She did the twist."

Mick shot me another look over Chrissie's bent head. It said *let's go!* in no uncertain terms.

"Um, Chrissie—" I started.

"Look at this one!" Chrissie pointed to another photo.

And so I had to look. And I had to look at the next page, and the next. We moved through local contests to statewide to regional. Her eighth year had been her best—she'd won a trip to Florida with her mom.

And then, suddenly, she began to get plump. I noticed that her hair was beginning to darken.

"The junior miss years were not her best." Chrissie sighed. "She just didn't work hard enough anymore. This year, she got Prettiest Dress. You should have seen the girl who won. No talent! Katie was robbed."

Finally, we reached the end of the album. "I've got more," Chrissie said hopefully.

"Gee," Mick said, "that sounds fantastic, but we really have to go."

"Oh. Yeah. I guess you have things to do." Chrissie looked disappointed, but she smiled at us. "You two sure make a cute couple."

"We're not a couple," I said quickly, before Mick could laugh, or hoot, *who, her?*

We stood up. Chrissie started to lead us to the door, but she stopped. "Do you want to see her room before you go, though? I decorated it myself."

We hesitated.

"Oh, come on. It will just take a minute," Chrissie said. "And maybe you can tell your moms about it. Word of mouth is the best way to build a business."

"Sure," I said.

Mick held on to the tail of my jacket as

Chrissie started for the stairs. "What are you doing to me?" he whispered.

"It will just take a minute," I said.

"When I told you to develop your people skills, I didn't have this in mind," he muttered as we started toward the stairs.

"At least I'm not telling Chrissie that she reminds me of my cousin Hassie," I hissed.

Hanging on the stairway wall was a gallery of photographs of Katie. Blond ringlets, pink lipstick, mascara, frothy gowns, cowgirl outfits, baton twirling. But I suddenly realized that nowhere in the house had I seen a recent picture of her. It was like she was frozen in her perfect blond childhood.

Katie's room was yellow and pink. There was daisy-patterned wallpaper and a matching headboard. Silk daisies were in a crystal vase on her dresser.

"I redecorated it for her sixteenth birthday. I wanted her to feel like she was sleeping in a meadow," Chrissie said proudly. "I thought it would cheer her right up. Bright colors cheer me up. I always wear a bright color on a rainy day."

Mick ran his hand along a part of the wall where the wallpaper was torn off.

"Oh, I keep meaning to fix that. Or at least hang a picture over it or something," Chrissie fretted. "That was her gallery wall. I framed all her sashes from her wins—you know, Little Princess of Oneonta, stuff like that—and some of her best studio photos, and hung them there. She took them all down one night and tore the paper. It's really good paper, too. I don't want to tell you what I paid. Hoo, boy. She hung a cheap poster over it."

I saw a poster rolled up in the corner, by the desk. All I could see were the eyes. A poster of some actress. The green eyes seemed to follow me as I crossed the room, like that guy on the billboard in *The Great Gatsby*, by F. Scott Fitzgerald. We'd read the book this year in English.

I suddenly thought of Camille. She had borrowed the book from me and never returned it. When I'd gotten an A on the essay test, she'd gotten a C minus. She blamed me because she said I should have helped her study. But she'd never even read the book. That was back when she was just starting to hang out with Mick's crowd.

I wrenched my attention back to Chrissie. She sat on the bed and smoothed the spread.

"She calls sometimes. She knows I worry. She was so young when she left. She took off. At first, I didn't know what happened to her. I went to the police and everything."

I shot a look at Mick.

"But she did call, finally. Said she had a job and an apartment, and I shouldn't worry. But she wouldn't tell me where she was."

Chrissie began to cry. I took a tissue from a box that was resting in a crocheted holder festooned with daisies. I handed it to her, and she blew her nose.

"She'll always be my baby," she said, looking up at us. Her mascara was smeared. "You'll tell her that, won't you?"

"If we see her, we'll tell her," I said.

"She's still pretty, you know," Chrissie said suddenly. "You can see that in her bone structure. It's like mine. She's a knockout, let me tell you. Even with that short haircut she gave herself. If she'd just *do* something with herself. When she was a teenager, I'd say, *honey, you've got to smile!* She resented all those lessons—the dancing lessons and the makeup lessons and the posture lessons. But she had to learn how to be graceful and feminine, didn't she? I didn't like her playing rough games with the kids around here. She was always meant for better things. And I think she'll thank me one day. I do." Chrissie blew her nose.

"I'm sure," I murmured, but Chrissie wasn't really talking to us.

"Maybe I shouldn't have remarried. It was always just me and my baby. She hated Vic. And sure, he turned out to be a bum. But he was real sweet to me in the beginning."

Chrissie stood up and straightened the bedspread. She moved jerkily, straightening a row of crystal figurines on the dresser, moving a lamp shade that had been perfectly straight.

"Then she even hated her name. After all the time I spent choosing it! I bought *four* baby name books. I made lists. . . . But when she was fifteen, she said she wanted to go by her initials. She was just selfish, that's all."

Chrissie pulled out a drawer and brought out a white envelope. I heard a jangle as she ripped the seal, as though it were filled with broken glass. She held out the envelope for us to see. Inside were smashed crystal daisies.

"I bought her these for her birthday, to go with her name. She smashed them all, right in front of my eyes. She left for good three days later." Chrissie's mascara-ringed eyes pleaded with us for understanding. "And she said *I* was the one who was crazy, that I gave her a stupid name. But wasn't it crazy for her to smash those pretty flowers like that?"

"I'm really sorry," I said.

The whole thing was so sad. But we were involved in our own sad story, and our time was short.

"Look, Chrissie," I said. "If we see Katie, we'll tell her that you miss her."

Chrissie put the envelope on the dresser. "Thank you."

She walked us downstairs. When we got to the front door, she turned to us. Her face was all red from crying, but she gave us a bright smile. "I must look a fright."

"You look just fine," Mick said. "Thank you for showing us the pictures."

We started down the walk. "Don't forget to tell your mothers about my decorating!" she yelled after us hopefully.

Mick started the car, and we drove off. "Wow," he said. "That was depressing."

"And we didn't learn anything," I said. "It's a weird coincidence that Katie ran away from home. But I don't think it connects her to Camille."

"With a mother like that, I'd be in Timbuktu," Mick said.

"We'll have to hook up with Katie at the mall tomorrow after all," I said. "Maybe we can get her to call her mom."

"Yeah," Mick said. "Maybe we can reunite Katie and Chrissie. But what about Camille?"

8//totally whacked

We were almost home when I remembered something. Those green eyes in the poster. Katie's poster had been of Deva Winter.

"Isn't that weird, Mick?" I said as we cruised down the state road. "Every time we turn around, we bump into Deva Winter."

"Are you saying she kidnapped Camille?" Mick asked sourly. Maybe he was still sore from a few minutes before, when I'd told him that he needed a refresher course in driver's ed.

I twisted around in my seat, or as much as I could with my shoulder harness on. "Andrew—if that's even his real name—mentioned Deva a bunch of times in the e-mail they exchanged. He first saw Camille at that look-alike contest. And Katie was there, too! Now I see a poster of Deva in Katie's room."

"If she's a fan, that makes perfect sense," Mick said. But he frowned, thinking. "And there's another coincidence. Deva is *here*—she's filming in Saratoga Springs, remember?"

"That's right," I said. "But what does it all *mean?*"

"I don't know," Mick said. "Maybe there's a connection somehow."

"Remember when Ronnie said that Deva was bothered by a stalker in L.A.?" I said.

Mick nodded.

"Hang on," I said slowly. "This might be totally whacked. But what if Deva Winter's stalker was *Andrew?* What if he went after Camille since she looks like Deva? He probably can't get near Deva—I bet she has bodyguards. But he can get the next best thing—"

"Camille," Mick breathed. "That does sound totally whacked. But maybe we should check it out."

"So what's the first step?" I asked.

Mick glanced at me. "Hey, you were on a roll. You tell me."

"I'm busted," I said. "Your turn."

Mick drove for a moment without speaking. "Okay," he said. "I've got a question. How did Andrew get Camille's e-mail address?"

"Excellent question," I approved. "And a good place to start."

The only possible connection between Andrew and Camille was still the Deva Winter Fan Club.

But this time, I had Mick call Ronnie.

"Because you made such an *impression*," I said.

Ronnie was delighted to hear from Mick. When he asked about mailing lists for the fan club, she was glad to give him an answer. I pressed against Mick as he talked so I could hear Ronnie.

"No problem," I heard her say.

Mick listened, nodding. "Bingo!" he said. "That's just what I wanted to hear. Hold on."

He covered the receiver and said, "Ronnie said the fan club has a Web site that lists online addresses for people who want to chat about Deva."

"That must be how she met Andrew," I said. "Camille's address is easy to figure out."

Mick nodded. "It's camiltano. He knew her full name, from the contest—"

"So when he accessed the Web site, he looked for an e-mail address that matched it," I finished.

We heard Ronnie's voice through the receiver, and Mick quickly put it back to his ear. "What was that, Ronnie? I missed it . . . oh. Well, I told you that Camille is missing, right? We just had this theory that this guy Andrew—that's not necessarily his real name—might be Deva's stalker."

Slowly, Mick's face changed. "Are you sure?"

"What?" I whispered.

"Okay," Mick said. I tugged at his sleeve.

Mick said good-bye and hung up. He looked dazed.

"Deva's stalker is a *girl,*" he said.

Mick and I chewed on this information like a piece of beef jerky. We didn't come up with any bright ideas. Then, after a while we heard banging and clanging from the kitchen. We were right next door, in the family room, so it sounded loud.

"Relax," I said, when Mick looked startled. "It's not a marching band tuning up. Mom and Dad are starting dinner prep. The kitchen is kind of small, so they always bump into each other and drop things. Then they get into a big discussion about what they'd do if they could afford to remodel. Then they argue about countertops and double sinks. I honestly don't know how we end up with a meal on the table."

Just then my little brother Doug cranked up the boom box in his room. Matt, who just got home from his pickup basketball game after work, started to sing in the shower. Then Alex bellowed, "I'm calling Melinda, so nobody pick up the phone for a half hour or you're *dead!*"

In other words, the Kurtz abode had clicked into normal mode.

"There's a window of time every afternoon when this house tends to explode," I told Mick. "But it usually quiets down again after dinner."

"It must be nice to live in a house with so much energy," Mick said.

"It sucks," I said.

Just then, Mom poked her head in the room. "Mick, want to stay for dinner?"

I gave her a *Mom!* look. Did she have to humiliate me that way?

She ignored me. "We're making Thai stir-fry."

"He can't—" I started.

"I'd love to," Mick said at the same time.

He looked at me. I glanced away, embarrassed. Mick had probably accepted because he thought it would be rude not to.

"Twenty minutes," Mom said. "If I can get your father to concentrate on chopping mushrooms instead of arguing with me about granite countertops."

"My parents take these night courses in cooking," I told Mick when Mom scurried back to the kitchen. "Their stir-fry is very spicy. I hope you brought some asbestos for your mouth. Anyway, they're pretty decent cooks."

I realized I was babbling, because Mick was staring at me.

"That's a bonus," he said. "But it's not why I stayed."

"Oh, right. I guess there's no sense wasting time," I said. "We can go online right after dinner and look up articles on the stalker."

Mick smiled faintly. I noticed that his eyes were the color of honey when the sun shines through the glass bottle. There was a darker spot of pigment in one of them, like a freckle.

"That's a good idea. But it's not why I stayed," he said.

My swallow seemed very loud. "Why did you stay, then?" I asked.

One corner of his mouth lifted. "Why do you think I did, Mina?" he asked softly. "You get one more guess."

Slowly, I became aware of something extraordinary. Mick Mahoney was flirting with me. And I wasn't good at this. He knew it. I could see by his smile. He was glad I was flustered. Maybe he was paying me back for all the smart remarks I'd made in the car. He was making fun of me.

My face flushed again. I turned away quickly. I would never, ever let Mick

Mahoney know that he'd gotten to me. For a second, I almost believed that he was flirting with me because . . . well, because he wanted to.

Which was pretty low, considering that the girl he was in love with was missing.

"I've got it. Because you like Thai food," I said.

After dinner, we commandeered the computer in the family room and sped through the Net. We found an L.A. newspaper with archives and we did a search on Deva's name.

Two articles on her stalker popped up. We accessed the first one, from six months before, called "Star Injured During Tussle with Fan."

It was about a seventeen-year-old girl named Kristle Pollack. A restraining order against the girl had been issued after she secretly moved into an outbuilding on Deva's property and monitored the actress's every move.

Kristle Pollack had violated the order. She'd hid in the backseat of Deva's car.

Deva had panicked when Kristle had popped up. She'd jammed on the brakes and hit a palm tree, which caused her head to hit the steering wheel. It was just a minor injury, but she'd tried to race away from the car, and Kristle had tackled her. People showed up and broke them apart. Deva got a sprained wrist, but she hadn't been hurt badly.

The next article was called "Deva Winter Appears in Court, Names Attacker."

It was a short article saying that a deal was made between Deva's lawyers and Kristle Pollack, and that Kristle had been released.

We downloaded a photo of the stalker, but it wasn't helpful. It was taken outside of the police station. A girl of medium height was running toward her car. She was wearing a baseball cap and sunglasses, and she had kept her head down, so we couldn't get a good look at her face.

"It could be anybody," I said.

"But she was arrested," Mick said, pointing at the screen. "So that means there was a mug shot, right?"

"I guess so," I said. "But she's a juvenile. Wouldn't the record be sealed?"

"Not to the police working the case here," Mick pointed out. "We've got to lay all this out for them. It doesn't add up to much, but maybe they can figure out a lead."

I looked at my watch. "It's only eight o'clock. Let's do it tonight."

We called Mrs. Brentano, who said that FBI Agent Tyson was at her house and we could talk to him about the case. So we drove over.

We started from the beginning and explained about the connections to Deva Winter, and how we'd thought that maybe her stalker had something to do with Camille's disappearance. Agent Tyson listened to us, but he didn't write anything down.

"We don't know how it all connects, but it seems like Deva Winter's name keeps popping up," I finished. "Maybe this girl Kristle Pollack is involved with Andrew somehow."

Agent Tyson nodded. "Thank you for your input," he said.

We waited, but he didn't say anything else. He didn't ask a question. Mrs. Brentano sat on the couch, smoking nervously. She'd quit smoking at least ten years ago.

"Is that it?" I asked.

"That's it," he said. "I'll make a report."

"But you don't think there's a connection?" I persisted.

He sighed. "Look. It's great that you kids want to find your friend. I admire that. But first of all, you're poking your nose into something that you should leave to professionals, okay? And second, I don't see the connection between a possible kidnapping and an overactive fan."

"She isn't a *fan*," Mick said. "She's a *stalker*."

"Right," Agent Tyson said. "Maybe. Or maybe it's a publicity stunt. A seventeen-year-old girl is a major threat to a star like Deva Winter? Give me a break. But say she is some kind of superfreak. You still haven't connected her to Camille."

"That's your job," Mick said, and Agent Tyson looked annoyed.

"Camille ran away," Mrs. Brentano said,

blowing out smoke. "She hasn't been kidnapped, all right? I'm sure she'll call, or she'll be found. Let the FBI do their job, Mina. They'll find her. She's trying to embarrass me. Or break up my engagement to Jonathan. The publicity has been awful. Everyone thinks I'm a bad mother. She wanted everyone to think that."

"Nobody thinks that, Elaine," Agent Tyson said gently.

Mrs. Brentano took a deep drag on her cigarette. A tear slowly snaked down her cheek. "She'll come home," she said.

I opened my mouth, but Agent Tyson put a hand on my arm.

"Let me walk you out," he said.

He brought us out to the porch. He fixed us with a flinty gaze. "Listen to me, kids. Your friend has possibly been abducted, right? This is serious business. If you come racing over here with every lamebrain theory you come up with, you're going to upset Mrs. Brentano. Is that what you want?"

"Of course not," I said.

"Right," Mick said angrily. "We wouldn't

want to mess up her engagement to van Veeder."

Agent Tyson stared at Mick for a long moment. "You don't know anything, kid," he said in a soft tone. "So watch what you say. Mrs. Brentano is upset right now. We've discovered that a convicted felon on parole was spotted at the mall that day."

"Convicted of what?" Mick asked.

"Abducting a young kid in Oregon," he answered. "This creep went to prison for twenty years, and he just got out. The police were lucky way back then—they found the kid when she was still alive. She was thirteen years old. He buried her in a box."

I gasped. Mick stiffened. We both stood there without saying a word. I felt my Thai stir-fry dinner turn over in my stomach.

"Does Mrs. Brentano know what he did?" I asked.

"Yes, she does. And she's not feeling real good at the moment. You see what I'm talking about?"

I nodded. "We don't want to make things worse."

"I was out of line," Mick said.

Agent Tyson's flinty look softened. "Okay. Listen, we're also still checking out that report of the teenage girl hitchhiking on the Taconic. We don't know anything yet. So go home, and wait. That's all you can do."

Mick and I walked slowly down the driveway to his car. We drove through the dark streets without saying anything.

"That's not all we can do," Mick said softly.

I waited.

"We can talk to Deva Winter herself," he said.

9//butterfly

From the electronic diary of BIGFAN#1

I'm really trying to be patient. But sometimes, I start to think that Camille isn't very nice. I try to talk to her about how we're both in show business, and how I won all those beauty pageants and so I know about competition, and do you know what she said? She said, "Where was the pageant? At the dog show?"

Now that's just mean. It made me mad. So I was already mad when I saw her ankle. Her sock had fallen down. She has a tattoo! *A butterfly. It's supposed to be pretty, but it's gross.*

Deva doesn't have any tattoos. Deva has perfect skin. All the makeup artists in Hollywood say so. They compare it to poured cream or moonlight on silk. Deva once said she'd never get a tattoo, because she changes her mind so much, and she'd probably decide that she hated it in a week. Besides, Deva isn't trendy. She's classic.

Camille saw me staring at it. She looked nervous. Then she started asking me about the pageants I was in. Like I believed she was really interested! I didn't answer her. I'm trying to figure out how to get rid of the tattoo. I know people go to doctors, but what do they do? Burn it off? Maybe you can scrape it off, if you rub it with something really scratchy, like steel wool? How many layers are there on your skin, anyway?

Something else to think about. My brain is starting to hurt, with all this thinking. I wish Camille would be nicer to me. This isn't working out at all. I thought we'd be friends by now.

10//star machinery

Mick was so convinced that he could get to Deva Winter that I assumed he had a foolproof plan. I asked him about it the next morning as we drove to Saratoga Springs.

"I don't have a plan," he said.

"You don't have a plan?" I yelled, clutching the door handle. We were going sixty, and the car felt as though it would blow apart any second. "Do you think we can just walk right up to Deva Winter on a movie set and say hi?"

"Sometimes the best plan is no plan," Mick answered calmly. "We have to be able to roll with the punches. Maneuver the curves. Go with the flow. Follow a hunch. Be brilliant."

"Or flirt with a gofer," I said.

"Precisely," Mick said.

##

Deva's movie, which had the awful title of *Autumn's Spring*—apparently, she was playing an 1890s card shark named Autumn Prendergast—was filming in an old Victorian mansion in Saratoga Springs. It was easy to find. All we had to do was ask at a gas station.

We spotted the location set from two blocks away. Long trailers were lined up on the street, and barricades closed off the sidewalk in front of the house. There were technicians doing something to lights, and people standing around drinking coffee. But we didn't see Deva, or any actors in nineteenth-century dress, so we figured they weren't shooting at the moment.

We hung behind the barricade with a group of curious onlookers. After a few minutes, someone would get bored and walk away, and someone else would take their place. Within a few minutes, we were pressed up against the barricade in front and were able to scope out the crew.

"Okay, big guy," I said to Mick. "We're clueless and planless. What do we do now?"

Mick didn't answer. He was staring off, and I followed his gaze. A girl a little older than us was drinking a bottle of Evian. She wore a baseball cap turned backward and hiking boots with a pair of cutoffs. She was cute, with curly dark hair and a slender, athletic body.

"Does she remind you of your cousin Hassie, by any chance?" I asked.

"Just hang out here a minute," Mick murmured.

But I disobeyed the order and followed behind him a few paces. I didn't want to cramp his style, but how could I resist checking out his moves?

I hung back while Mick approached the crew member. She seemed standoffish at first, but I saw the beginnings of a smile as Mick said something. Then he leaned in closer, and she laughed.

"Oh, brother," I muttered. I walked closer.

"No exceptions," the girl was saying as I got within earshot.

"How about a note?" Mick asked. "Come on, Rebecca. Give a guy a break, will you? Every aspiring journalist needs one."

"No notes," the girl said. "Picture a moat and a drawbridge, okay? When it comes to Deva Winter, the drawbridge is always up. And I'm just a lowly P.A. I don't get near the princess."

"You might be a lowly P.A. now," Mick said. "But you're going to be a famous director one day. Am I right?"

Rebecca looked pleased. "Yeah, I hope so."

Mick took a step closer. "Look," he said in a persuasive tone. "I won't tell her who helped me. I promise." He scribbled something on a piece of paper. "Just give her this. And someday, when I'm writing for *The New York Times*, I'll review your movie."

Rebecca grinned. "I don't believe a word you're saying." But when Mick handed her the note, she took it. "I'll give it to Tom, the wardrobe assistant. Maybe he'll pass it along to Deva's assistant, Jennifer. But that's all I'm going to do. No matter how much you flash that dimple at me, pretty boy." She reached out and touched the dimple in the side of Mick's cheek.

"Be still, my heart," Mick said. "I've just been touched by an angel."

She rolled her eyes, but she grinned. She walked off toward the trailers, and I stepped up next to Mick.

"I've really got to pack some antacids next time," I said. "My stomach just can't take this."

"Would you lighten up, Kurtz?" Mick asked, his eyes on Rebecca as she picked her way across cables. "If we get to see Deva Winter, I'll buy you a case of antacids, okay?"

We waited by the barricade for about fifteen very long minutes. Finally, a lanky guy with a clipboard came out from a trailer and walked toward us.

"Mick Mahoney?"

Mick nodded.

"Follow me."

We squeezed between the barricades and followed the lanky guy. He led us to a long trailer, knocked on the door, and disappeared.

The door swung open. A woman with red hair and black-framed glasses stood there. "So?" she said. She seemed to bristle at the sight of us.

"So?" Mick said.

"Why do you have to see Ms. Winter right now? Can't you set up an appointment to interview her like other reporters do?" she asked.

"Can we come inside?" Mick asked.

She hesitated. "For a minute."

Inside, the trailer was like an expensively decorated living room. There was a plush gray carpet, and a sofa upholstered in deep plum velvet. Chrome chairs with maroon leather seats were pulled up around a burnished wood worktable. A patterned velvet curtain in soft grays hung in the hall, shielding the rest of the trailer.

"I'll get right to the point," Mick said.

"I'd appreciate it," the woman said crisply. She folded her arms.

"I'm not really a reporter," Mick said. "Our friend is missing, and the FBI thinks she's been abducted. We have reason to believe that the girl who stalked Deva might be involved. Kristle Pollack."

"So why are you here?" the woman rapped out. She didn't even say she was sorry to hear about Camille's disappearance.

"We'd like to talk to Deva, if we could," Mick said. He kept his voice level, but I knew the woman's rudeness was irritating him. "We'd like to ask her some questions, maybe get a few details from her, things the press doesn't know about. Something for us to go on. Do you think Deva would give us five minutes?"

"Absolutely not," the woman snapped. "The subject of Kristle Pollack is off-limits with Deva Winter. She's been through enough."

"Then why did you see us?" Mick countered. "Deva must be concerned. What if Kristle is in the area?"

"Impossible," the woman replied. But she looked nervous. "She was paid a great deal of money to stay away. She signed an agreement—"

"She's a *stalker*," I burst out. "I'm no criminologist, but I know that stalkers don't just 'stay away.' Our friend Camille is missing. And just weeks ago, she won a Deva Winter look-alike contest—"

We heard a rustle of movement, and the curtain was swept back. Deva Winter stood in the hallway. She was dressed in a white gown with a bustle, in the style of the 1890s. Instead of her signature short, feathered cut, a wig that exactly matched her glossy dark hair flowed down to her waist. She was astonishingly beautiful.

No one spoke. Her large, luminous green eyes studied us warily. "Did you say your friend was missing?" she asked.

11//close to you

I nodded.

"And we're hoping that you can help us," Mick said gently.

Deva didn't let go of the curtain. Her slender hand clutched it as though she were afraid, or nervous.

"I got a letter from Kristle," she said. "She's not supposed to contact me, but she did. I don't know how it slipped through, because Jennifer"—and she pointed with her chin at the redhaired woman—"opens all my mail. It was slipped in with the pile that had been opened. There was no stamp or postmark, so it had been hand-delivered. I just thought that Jennifer had overlooked it. Kristle said something about forging a bond with a new friend. She said that soon I'd know how she could take care of someone." Deva shuddered. "She said . . . 'she's as close to you as I can get. For now.'"

"Do you have the letter?" I asked.

She shook her head. "I gave it to the police, and they forwarded it to the officer in L.A. who's handling my case."

"What about the e-mails that Kristle sent you?" Mick asked. "Do you have those?"

"I—I guess they're still on my hard drive," Deva said hesitantly.

"Could you send us copies?" Mick asked.

"I don't know," Deva murmured.

"We have to ask Ronald about that," Jennifer spoke up.

"Ronald handles my security," Deva said.

"We just want to see if we can find some clues," Mick said. "If Kristle has something to do with Camille's disappearance, then the police will really have something on her. That could be good for you, too."

"You don't know what it's like," Deva said. Her fingers crushed the velvet of the curtain, then relaxed. She looked away from us, out the window. "People think I made too much of it. That I'm high-strung. But the girl is crazy. Nobody believes how crazy she is. And the police can't do anything. She hasn't physically harmed me. *I'm* the one who crashed the car into a tree. She tackled me, but she told people I was about to run into traffic. She never broke a law until she trespassed on my property that time. She sends me presents. She finds out where I am. She reads every single thing that's written about me. She knows what Internet chat rooms I visit and haunts them. I think it's how she finds out my e-mail address." She turned her face to us. A beam of sunlight hit her eyes, turning them aquamarine. "Do you really think she's here?" she whispered.

"We don't know," Mick said.

"That's enough," Jennifer said crisply. "Deva, you need to have food and rest. This is too upsetting. You two need to leave."

Quickly, Mick reached for a pad and pushed it toward me with a pen. "Mina will write down her e-mail address. You can just send the letters that way. We'd really, really appreciate it."

"She's crazy, you know," Deva said. "I've seen her in person, talked to her. She's crazy."

Deva faded back, letting the curtain fall. She'd been more like an apparition than a person.

"Good-bye, then," Jennifer said, in no uncertain terms.

Mick pushed the pad toward her in a mute entreaty. Then we hurried out of the trailer.

We'd only gone a few steps when Rebecca charged toward us. She hit Mick with the palms of both hands on his chest. He staggered backward. "You snake!" she yelled. "You slime! You and your dimples!"

"Hey! What's the matter?" Mick asked as she hit him again.

"I just got fired, that's what happened!" Rebecca shouted. "Not only me, but my friend who passed Jennifer the note. Thanks a lot, buddy!"

"Rebecca, I didn't tell her," Mick said. "I promise—"

She flung her hands in the air, as if to say, *so what?* Then she spun around, her curls flying, and gestured at Deva's trailer. "That's what a witch she is," she hissed. Then she stalked off.

"No," I said softly, staring at Deva's trailer. "That's how scared she is."

12//betrayal

From the electronic diary of BIGFAN#1

How could she do this to me? How could she! I kept her warm, and fed her, and even let her look out the window once. She said she wanted to see the river. We were getting to be friends! She even promised to go with me to get the tattoo off. She said that would be okay, that she hated it, too. Some mean boyfriend made her do it. We were bonding! I was so happy that I even wrote Deva, and I promised myself I wouldn't do that if I wasn't sure that Camille and I were best friends.

But she tried to get away. She rushed at me and knocked me down. Now I know that she got this rusty piece of metal—a piece of some old machine, and I swept this place out a gazillion times!—and just kept sawing away at the ropes.

I had to hit her. I tried not to hurt her! But she was hitting me! Then she fell, and she hit her head. I heard it go crack.

I didn't want her to bleed. I didn't want her to hurt. Now she's so quiet. I think she's hurt bad. She's breathing. But she sounds weak. What should I do? This is all her fault! It's all her fault! Now I really can't let her go. Deva wouldn't understand.

Now I can't let her go. What am I going to do? Deva!

13//hang on

"You're awfully quiet," Mick said over the sound of the engine on the drive home.

I stared out at the green trees rushing by. "I have a bad feeling, Mick," I said. "Time feels like it's running out."

Back in Saratoga Springs, we had called the number Agent Tyson had given us. We'd given the FBI the information about Deva's stalker. There really wasn't anything else we could do.

Mick nodded grimly. "I have the same feeling. That's why we have to keep going. Okay. Let's just go over this. If this girl Kristle was involved, how did she hook up with Andrew? Through the fan club? Or did they meet in California, then come out here together?"

"What difference does it make?" I asked

tiredly. I rested my forehead against the window. The glass felt cool against my hot forehead.

"If they don't know the area, it would be hard to figure out where to keep her, I guess," Mick said. "Let's face it. Every town near Mohawk Falls has an abandoned building, or a factory, or a farm—"

"Exactly," I said. "That's why the FBI has such a big job. There are hundreds of places they could hide her. If they even stayed in the area."

The landscape rushed by. Spring starts slowly in upstate New York. But once it arrives, it knocks you over the head. In just the last few days, everything had started to bloom. The trees were full of tender green leaves, and the shrubs along the highway were a blaze of yellow. If Camille was being held somewhere, did she get to go outside and smell the spring?

"How did they do it, Mick?" I asked softly. "Do you think Camille knew she was being kidnapped? They must have tricked her. She must have gone willingly, at first. How else did they get her to leave the mall?"

"Wait a second," Mick said. He hit the steering wheel. "We're assuming that Andrew is a *guy*. What if Andrew is Kristle? What if she assumed that name online, just to get close to Camille?"

Slowly, I straightened. "That's definitely possible," I said. "You can be anybody you want online. And Camille said she hadn't even spoken to Andrew on the phone. So it could be Kristle. But why would Camy take off with her? I mean, *Camille*. You know, I don't understand why Camille hates that nickname. It's so hard to change when you've been calling someone by a name their whole life. And it's not like it's Fatso, or Dumpy—"

Suddenly, I stopped. I'd just had a totally genius idea.

"Mina?"

I pounded the dashboard with my fists excitedly.

"Hey! I wouldn't do that if I were you. We might lose a wheel." Mick gave me a brief glance. "What is it?"

"Nicknames!" I said. I squirmed in the seat, trying to reach into the back pocket of my jeans. I took out a crumpled piece of paper and scanned it.

"I got it wrong, Mick," I said, waving the paper at him. "The yogurt girl who wrote out the address wrote it on the back of this slip of paper. I never looked at the front, where she wrote Katie's name."

"So?" Mick asked, frowning at the road.

"It's not Katie—it's K. D.!" I crowed.

"Kady?" Mick asked.

"No, the initials—K. D.," I said.

"Okay," Mick said slowly. "Call me stupid. I'm still not getting it."

"Remember what Chrissie said?" I reminded him. "Her daughter hated her name and went by her initials! And remember her room? There was a major daisy motif. The wallpaper. The headboard. And the crystal flowers that Katie smashed. Crystal daisies—get it? Crystal is spelled with a 'K.' *Kristle Daisy* is her name. K. D."

"Wait a second." Mick swept his hair back from his forehead. "You said Katie—I mean, K. D.—was stocky, and dark."

"And that's why Chrissie doesn't have any pictures of her past the age of ten or twelve," I said. "Remember, she said she was still pretty? Didn't she sound defensive? She said she had good *bone structure*. You know what that means."

"It's like saying a girl has a good personality," Mick said, nodding. "As the guys in our class would say, Woofburger Alert."

"And there were initials stamped in gold on the photo album," I said, remembering. "K. D. P."

"Chrissie's last name is Farmer," Mick said.

"Chrissie married again, remember?" I said. "K. D. probably kept her old name. She hated her stepfather."

"So Deva's stalker is our yogurt girl," Mick said. "She *is* in the neighborhood. We have to tell the FBI."

"And Deva," I said.

He glanced at me. "It's Thursday."

I looked at my watch. "And it's four-thirty. She's at work. Let's go."

We raced through the mall toward the food court. A girl with curly blond hair was manning the counter. We stopped at the water fountain until we could breathe normally. We watched the yogurt shop for ten minutes, but there was no sign of K. D.

Finally, we walked up. We ordered two frozen yogurts with bananas.

Mick paid the girl. He smiled. "Hey, is K. D. around, by any chance? I think she works tonight, right?"

The girl shook her head. "Not anymore. She doesn't work here at all. She quit this morning. Talk about last minute."

"Oh," Mick said. "Thanks, anyway."

We walked away. We threw our yogurts in the trash.

"Mick . . . ," I said.

"I know," he said in a flat tone.

"I feel so helpless," I said.

"We've got to hang on," Mick said. His soft golden eyes met mine. "Because somewhere, Camille is."

14//the river is soft

From the electronic diary of BIGFAN#1

The river is soft, so soft. In the dark, it's like velvet. And it's cool and restful.

It holds you and cradles you, like the mother you never had. It tells you that you're perfect the way you are. You don't need to worry anymore. Everything bad is behind you. The words whisper over pebbles and sand. "Rest now. Rest now."

The river murmurs those words, and you slip into it, and your eyes are open, staring at the stars. And someone closes your eyes, and lets you go.

And the river says: Ah. Here you are. Let me hold you. Let me rock you forever in my soft, soft arms.

15//the worst never happens

Mick and I decided to head back to my house. We'd check my e-mail to see if Deva had sent those letters, and then Mick would head home. We were both bushed.

Mick still wasn't totally convinced that K. D. was Kristle. The initials could be a coincidence, he kept saying. If only we had a photograph!

"We've got to call the FBI again," I said as we pulled into my driveway.

Mick sighed as he turned off the engine. "I'm not looking forward to it. They keep treating us like idiots."

"But they do listen," I said. "And we have no choice."

Just then, Mom came out of the house. She stood on the front steps, waiting for us.

I started to wave, but my hand faltered when I saw her face.

And then my heart seemed to stop beating. "Something's wrong," I said.

My fingers fumbled with the door handle. I ran, stumbling, toward the house. Mick was right behind me.

"Mom?" I said.

She put her hands on my shoulders. "They found a body," she said.

They'd found it in the reeds, at the river's edge. It had been weighted with stones so that it would sink, but the current was too strong. The body fit Camille's description, but the white T-shirt and jeans she was wearing were generic. So there was still hope. They needed a positive I.D. from Camille's parents.

Dad drove us to Mrs. Brentano's house. My parents were silent. I guess we were all hoping. Praying.

Mrs. Brentano hadn't left for the morgue yet. They hadn't transported the body of the girl, who I kept telling myself over and over again was *not* Camille.

Camy's mom paced around the living room while Mr. Brentano sat on the couch, holding hands with his wife. Jonathan van Veeder sat in an armchair, looking lost.

"I know it isn't her, Sarah," Mrs. Brentano said to Mom as we walked in. "I know it."

Mom just hugged Mrs. Brentano. She rocked her a little, the way she used to rock me when I was younger.

Two policemen came into the house without knocking. They whispered something to the detective, who was standing with the FBI agents.

"What is it?" Mrs. Brentano started toward them. "Did you find something?"

"We're ready to go, Mrs. Brentano," one of the agents said gently.

"Oh." Mrs. Brentano said the word in a rush of breath. "But I can't," she said numbly. She backed away. Her knees hit a chair, and she fell into it. "I can't."

Mr. Brentano stood up. "Can't you tell us if she resembles Camille?" he asked hoarsely. "Can't you rule out that it's her? Do you have to put us through this?"

The detectives and agents exchanged glances. Then Agent Tyson, who had spent the most time with Mrs. Brentano, knelt by her chair.

"Does your daughter have a tattoo, Elaine?" he asked her gently. "On her ankle?"

Mrs. Brentano looked up. Tears had streaked her makeup. Her smile was radiant. "No!" she cried, relieved. "Of course she doesn't. Camille wouldn't—"

Mick reached for my hand. He squeezed it hard, and it hurt. But I didn't care. We held on to each other tightly.

I had to force the words out, as though I couldn't get enough air. "What is it a tattoo of?" I asked Agent Tyson.

He looked at me. I noticed for the first time that his eyes were blue, and ringed with bristly black lashes. I saw that his gaze was full of sudden knowledge, and swift compassion.

I knew it was over, then.

"A butterfly," he said.

16//the coldest rain

It rained on the day of Camille's funeral. A cold, steady rain that fell in sheets and never let up. The sky was a dull pewter color without even a sheen of pearl.

Isn't it seriously strange how sometimes the weather can cooperate with life, and become a big stage set for tragedy?

If I sound a little callous, it's because nothing felt real. It felt like a play, and we were just actors, not real people. And any minute Camille would burst through the door and say, "*Fooled ya! Wasn't it a gas?*"

The days before the funeral passed in slow motion. Every time I met someone, like a store clerk, or the mailman, I would want to say to the stranger taking my money, or handing me mail, *my best friend died this week.* I just couldn't believe that people could continue to deliver mail, hand me change, say, "Have a nice day," while somewhere, Camille lay dead. It seemed like the world should pause, or something.

The funeral was awful. I couldn't seem to connect the casket in the church with Camille. Her stupid friends, like Gigi and Pauline, kept heaving these loud, theatrical sobs that echoed in the church. I wanted to stuff their wet tissues in their mouths.

Mick sat across the aisle with his mother. He'd introduced me to her on the church steps. She looked like him, with sad golden eyes, and wheat-colored hair tucked underneath a black beret.

We followed the hearse to the graveyard. Everyone had black umbrellas except for Mick. His was red. I kept my eyes on it during the service. My mom and dad and three brothers were near the front. They left a place for me, but I hung back, near the rear. I had this cheap collapsible umbrella that kept threatening to turn inside out in the wind. I had to hold on to the spokes with one hand.

I didn't want to cry. I looked at the dirt

mounded up around the deep hole. It was turning into mud. I couldn't imagine Camille lying underneath all that mud. Didn't want to.

They said she died of a head injury. She didn't drown. She was already dead. She didn't have many bruises, so they didn't think she'd been mistreated. They told us that to make us feel better.

But her hair was all cut off. Her beautiful dark hair. Mrs. Brentano told me that, crying and crying, sobbing on my shoulder and saying, "My baby, my baby," over and over again, until I thought I'd howl it along with her.

At the graveside, Mrs. Brentano leaned on her fiancé Jonathan. He kept handing her fresh handkerchiefs. He looked kind and bewildered. I wanted to say to Camille, *Hey, Weasel Nose doesn't seem so bad after all. Give him a chance. He stuck by your mom.*

Mr. Brentano stood with his wife and her two young daughters. They looked pale and upset. I remembered how they used to torture Camy, read her diary, steal her underwear and hide it. I remembered the time Mr. Brentano forgot Camy's fifteenth birthday. I remembered how his wife always baked cakes for her daughters' birthdays, but always got a store-bought one for Camy.

Camille's grandmother had flown in from Arizona. I'd met her a couple of times. I know she loved Camille, but when Camille went out to visit, she told me that her grandmother took off and played golf all day. She didn't know what to do with her.

Gigi let out another dramatic, wracking sob. She leaned on her friend Pauline. I remembered when Camille and Gigi were on the outs, because Gigi had a crush on Mick when Camille began to date him. Gigi had organized all the girls to stop talking to Camille for about a week. Then she caved because Mick's band was playing in this all-day concert with a bunch of other bands, and Gigi really wanted to go.

Why hadn't I cajoled Camille that day at the mall? Why hadn't I remembered how to say, *Come on, Camy. Don't be mad. Plus, you hate the bus. I'll give you a ride.*

How strange it must be, to be buried, and all around you people were crying, and each and every one of them had let you down.

The priest finished. Gigi croaked what I hoped would be her last sob.

The casket was polished dark wood. A huge arrangement of pink and white flowers hung over it and trailed in the mud. Camille would have hated it. She never liked pink.

And remembering that, my eyes suddenly filled with hot tears. I balled my fist and pressed it against my mouth. My sob was deep and silent and wrenched my insides. My whole body seemed to crack open.

The priest told the soul of Camille Elise Brentano to rest in peace. Mrs. Brentano placed a rose on the casket.

Everyone had a rose, I saw. They filed by the casket, one by one, and placed the flower on it. Then they slogged through the muddy grass toward their cars.

My hands were empty. Someone had passed out roses, and I hadn't gotten one. I felt awful. I wanted to put a rose on Camille's casket. I wanted to say that private good-bye.

I felt a hand on my sleeve. It was Mick. He handed me a single white rose. We were the last ones at the grave. Together, we walked forward. I placed it on Camille's casket.

"Mick?"

We turned around. Gigi stood a few feet away, clutching her tissue. "Are you coming?" she called.

Mick looked at me. Then he slipped his arm around me. "I'm staying with Mina," he said.

Gigi's mouth dropped open. Then she shrugged, as if she didn't care, and walked away.

Mick and I walked toward his car, our umbrellas colliding with every step. We walked quickly over the slippery grass, so that we wouldn't have to hear the casket being lowered into the wet, black earth.

I really don't know if I could have made it through that awful day without Mick. His mom got a ride home, and Mick drove me to Mrs. Brentano's, where people were gathered. He found chairs for us against the wall. He brought me a cup of coffee and I drank it, even though I don't like coffee. He brought me a sandwich, and when I only took a bite, he didn't tell me to finish it.

We didn't talk. We just sat. People came over to say things to us, sympathetic things about how close we were to Camille, and how shocking it was to lose her. Mrs. Brentano thanked us in a numb voice for being there.

Nothing helped. Nothing mattered.

Finally, people began to go. Mom leaned over and murmured to me, "We should leave now, honey. Mrs. Brentano needs to rest. Jonathan is going to stay with her, and her mother is spending the night."

I glanced at Mick, and he nodded.

"I'm going to hang out with Mick for a while," I told Mom. "We're going to take a drive."

Mom gave Mick a smile. "Okay. Be careful. And do me a favor, okay? Be home for dinner tonight."

"I'm not hungry," I said.

"I don't care," Mom said gently. She put

a hand on my shoulder. "You don't have to eat. Just come home."

So I promised I would. The rain had slowed to a drizzle as Mick and I walked to the Volkswagen.

Mick drove carefully along the wet, black streets. Leaves were plastered to the car, and they stuck to the road, making slippery patches. It was only four o'clock, but it was close to dark, and Mick turned on the headlights. I heard thunder rumble from far away. The storm was moving on.

Mick drove aimlessly for a while. Then, we passed the high school. He pulled into the parking lot. He glided to a stop in the exact middle of the lot. He turned off the lights. We stared straight ahead at the school.

"Have you gone over and over what we've done since she disappeared?" I asked him. "Are you thinking that we should have been smarter, or figured things out faster?"

"Only every minute," Mick said. "Do you think we'll ever forgive ourselves, Mina?"

"I don't know," I said. "I can't imagine what forgiveness feels like."

"You tried so hard to find her," Mick said.

"So did you."

"So why do we feel so guilty?"

I sighed. "I haven't told anyone this, Mick. It's really been eating at me. Camille and I had a fight that day at the mall. She left because she was angry at me. If I had been nicer, I would have driven her home. And none of this would have happened."

Mick twisted in his seat. "Mina, that's crazy," he said. "It could have happened anytime. We think she was kidnapped by Deva's stalker, right? We know how stalkers work. They wait, and they watch."

"I guess so," I said.

"Let's take a walk," he said.

The drizzle had turned into a fine mist. It clung to our hair and our skin as we struck out across the parking lot, heading for the grassy quad.

The grass was slick and wet. We sat down in the middle of the lawn, getting our good clothes damp. But the grass smelled so fresh, and the water, when I ran my hands along the blades, felt cool. I touched a drop to my lips and swallowed.

"I haven't told anybody this, either," Mick said. "I broke up with Camille the night before she disappeared."

I turned and stared at him. He squinted across the lawn to the school.

"She went ballistic. She refused to accept it. She said we needed a 'cooling-off period.' But I stuck to my guns. I said no. I said it was over, period. We fought about it. Which shouldn't surprise me, since all we ever did was fight. Why shouldn't we do the same thing when we broke up?"

"She never mentioned it that day," I said. "But she did seem upset, I guess." And she was already talking about another guy.

"Here's the part I feel the most guilty about," Mick said. He hugged his knees. "I never loved her, Mina. I know we were supposed to be the perfect couple and everything. And all my guy friends envied me. She's so pretty—*was* so pretty. . . . But we never had anything to say to each other, somehow. And she needed me so much. She was always fighting with her mother, or angry at her father. And she really thought Gigi was lame. They weren't that close. I don't think she had a friend, except for you. And she blew you off. I think she was lonely, actually."

I thought about what Mick said. How guilty he felt. But over and over, I couldn't stop thinking *he never loved her*.

And it made me glad.

How's that for guilt?

Mick tore out a chunk of grass and threw it. "So if I hadn't broken up with her, maybe *I* would have been with her that day. She never would have gone to the mall. I'm the one who could have saved her."

I threw myself back on the wet grass. I looked up at the dark gray sky. "If we could go back and fix things, life would be some kind of rehearsal, not the real thing," I said.

He lay flat on his back beside me. "I think she missed you," he said. "But she wasn't strong enough to buck Gigi and that crowd. She liked all that attention. She liked being the big shot."

"Did you know that Camille had two of everything?" I asked. "Two sets of clothes and two sets of schoolbooks and two tooth-brushes—one for her mom's house, and one for her dad's. She was always split between them. They used to argue through her when she was little. But neither of them paid much attention to her. I guess that's why she liked hanging out at my house. It's always so noisy. And sometimes, Camy could be a spoiled brat with her mom. She never could get away with anything in my house. My brothers wouldn't let her."

"Sometimes she seemed to hate her dad," Mick said.

"When he got remarried, he suddenly didn't have much time for her anymore. He had two stepkids, and Camy felt that he gave them all his attention. There just wasn't much room for Camy there. That's what she said. She stopped going every weekend. I think she did it so that he'd force her to keep coming. But he never said anything. Maybe that's when she started to change. She got so unhappy."

Mick flipped over to face me. His white shirt was wet. Beads of moisture clung to his dark blond hair. "Do you think we all let her down?"

I nodded.

"So do I. Poor Camille."

Finally, finally, I started to cry. Tears started falling down my cheeks, faster and faster.

Mick's face creased with concern. "Mina—"

"It's okay," I said. "Really. I'm already wet."

He let out a choked sound, something like a laugh. Then he drew me to him fiercely. I put my arms around him, and we held each other as the mist fell and the smell of the grass and the earth surrounded us on this cold, wet day. We cried into each other's hair. We felt the softness of the rain on our skin. And our friend was dead.

17//square one

Everyone left the house early the next morning. Mom and Dad went to the nursery. Matt went to work. Alex took off for the day with his new girlfriend. And Doug went to the mall with his friend Scott.

Which left me alone, sitting at the kitchen table, in my robe. Clutching a hot mug of tea. Taking a sip. Nibbling on toast. Wondering what to do next. School would start again the next day, but my parents said I didn't have to go back right away if I didn't want to, which was really cool of them. It was just too strange to think of my life returning to normal, especially since this huge piece of it would be gone.

I heard a tap on the kitchen door and I looked up to see Mick standing outside. I'd never been so glad to see anyone in my life.

I hurried to the door and opened it.

"You look sleepy," he said.

"Don't you ever say hello?" I said. It was strange to see him after the night before, when we'd been lying on the grass together in the rain.

I tugged my white chenille bathrobe closer. I hadn't brushed my hair this morning, and I knew it was probably a mess, straggling down my back. "I overslept. Do you want some tea, or orange juice? And there's toast."

"O.J. would be great," Mick said. "Thanks."

I poured him a glass. We sat across the table from each other. The sun shone through the window and pooled on the old farm table, highlighting the honey-colored wood. I felt a stirring of something like pleasure as I cupped my hands around my mug. Then I felt a pang of guilt. The funeral had been only yesterday, and already, today, I was happy to be having breakfast with Camille's ex-boyfriend.

"I thought of a way to forgive ourselves," Mick told me.

"How?" I asked.

"Not give up. Look, maybe we were too late to catch Camille's kidnapper," Mick said. "But we could try to catch her killer."

"How?" I asked. "We reached a dead end. We've told the FBI everything we found out."

Before the funeral, we'd told the FBI about the possible Kristle-K. D. connection. But we hadn't heard anything since.

"Have you checked your e-mail lately?" he asked.

I started to shake my head, then looked at him. "Deva."

We took off for the family room, and I switched on the computer. My mail flag popped up, and it was from Jennifer, Deva's assistant. She'd forwarded Kristle's e-mail after all.

I scrolled through it. Mick read it over my shoulder. Then we got to the last paragraph of her final e-mail.

But don't be jealous. She'll be just like you . . .

I touched the computer screen. "The FBI should see this."

"Yeah," Mick said.

"I can be dressed in two seconds," I said.

We drove to the FBI office, and Agent Tyson saw us right away. We gave him a hard copy of the e-mail, and he scanned it.

"We already have this," he said. "Deva Winter sent it to us, too."

"So you think there's a connection?" I asked.

He sighed. "Look, kids," he said. "What happened to your friend was terrible. And I'm sorry. But the best thing you can do for her is go home. We'll catch the person. That's our job." He pointed to the papers. "We're checking out your crazy Deva Winter connection, okay?"

"What about the ex-con at the mall?" Mick asked.

"We located him. He's got an ironclad alibi. So yes, we're following your lead. I'm telling you this so that you'll leave it alone." Agent Tyson gave us both a stern look. "This could be dangerous. Let the pros handle it. You hear me?"

"We hear you," I said.

Mick was staring at Agent Tyson's waste-basket, as though he was embarrassed to be there at all. "We hear you," he said.

As we walked out, Mick pointed to the newspaper in Tyson's wastebasket. "You done with this?"

"Sure, take it," Tyson said tiredly. "And don't come back, okay?"

We hit the street and started walking toward the parking lot where we'd left the car.

"Well, I guess we should just head home," I said.

Mick was studying the lifestyles page of the paper. "Mmm."

"The FBI seems to be on top of it," I said. "I wish there was something more we could do, though."

"We could go back to square one," Mick said. "Back to the beginning. Where the whole thing started."

"Huh?" I looked at him, puzzled.

We stopped. Mick thrust the newspaper in my hands. He pointed to an article called "Star Does the Springs."

I scanned the article. It was one of those puff pieces on a celebrity—Deva. The local reporter got to hang out with a star and gush about how natural she was. Deva praised the town and said what a wonderful experience it had been filming there, even though she probably barely went out of her trailer and her hotel. Her favorite thing to do in Saratoga Springs was to take a mineral bath in the town's fizzy mineral springs. Naturally, Deva didn't head for the state park along with the masses. She went to the ritziest spa in town.

"Okay," I said. "I know that Deva likes to take mineral baths, and thinks the seaweed wrap is the best she's ever had. So?"

"Let's get into the mind of a stalker for a minute," Mick said. "She does something outrageous to get her idol's attention. It backfires. She was trying to show the star how she could protect her, and she ends up killing the person she kidnapped."

I winced. The "person" was Camille. "Keep going," I said.

"Okay," Mick said. "Wouldn't the stalker want to get to the star, explain what happened? In her own twisted way, of course. I bet Kristle is dying to see Deva now, talk to her." He pointed to the paper. "And now she knows how to get to her. *Spas don't have security checks, Mina.*"

"So you want to trap Kristle," I said slowly. "But how? Deva made it clear that she wouldn't help us anymore. If she was scared before, now she must be terrified."

"I wasn't thinking of Deva," Mick said. "I was thinking of a decoy. Someone who looks like her. Or, at least, someone who could pass for her."

"Great idea," I said, handing back the paper to Mick. "But where are you going to find such a person? I mean, Deva Winter is incredibly beautiful. She's also got amazing style. You just don't see girls like her walking down the street every day."

"Don't be so modest," Mick said.

It took me several very long seconds to put together what Mick had just said. Then I saw the look in his eyes.

"Me?" I squeaked.

18//game for anything

While we drove north, Mick assured me that his plan wouldn't be dangerous. He'd never put me in that position. He'd be watching me every minute.

"We'll be wired with cell phones," he told me.

"Mick, we don't have cell phones," I said.

"Just leave it to me," he said. "All we have to do is wait for Kristle to show up. She'll probably stake out the place—she won't even go inside. She'll wait for Deva, hoping she can ambush her. Meanwhile, the FBI arrives. Simple."

"It does sound simple," I said dubiously. "But a lot could go wrong."

"We'll make sure it doesn't," Mick assured me.

"How?"

He took the turnoff for Saratoga Springs. "We're going to take a tour of the place, figure everything out."

"Okay," I said. "Maybe we can make a foolproof plan for trapping her. But you're forgetting the most important detail. Look, I'm game for anything. I want to catch this girl. But how am I supposed to impersonate Deva Winter? It's impossible!"

Mick only smiled. "Just leave it to me," he said.

The spa was in the older section of town, in an old Victorian hotel. We parked across the street and looked at it.

"There's an ice-cream shop right across the street with a perfect view of the door," Mick said, pointing. "If I was going to stake out the place, that's where I'd sit. That's where Kristle can watch the front door."

"But how will she know when Deva is coming?" I asked.

"We'll make the appointment in Deva's name," Mick said. "We know the name of her assistant. You can pretend to be Jennifer."

"Okay," I said. "But how would Kristle find out when Deva's appointment is?"

Mick shrugged. "Maybe it's on computer. Maybe she hacks in. Or maybe she tricks them and peeks at the book. Kristle is resourceful. She managed to get Deva's e-mail address twice," he pointed out. "She got a letter to her, too. But even if she can't find it out, maybe she'll stake out the place. We can go every day at the same time, if we have to. But I don't think we'll have to."

Mick turned to me, his hand on the handle of the door. "Ready for a tour?"

"I always wanted a seaweed wrap," I said. "Whatever that is."

We told the girl at the front desk that we were tourists, thinking of making day appointments. We'd like a tour. No problem.

The spa was gorgeous, with bleached hardwood floors and blinding white paint. New Age music was piped in through loudspeakers, and the air smelled pleasantly of citrus and spice.

"Aromatherapy," our tour guide said.

She brought us to the mineral baths, the

sauna, and the steam room. She showed us the treatment rooms, the dressing rooms, and the "de-stress environment room." But Mick and I were more interested in places where someone could sneak in, or hide. We noted closets, private offices, and exit doors.

When we returned to the front desk, we made appointments, just to see how they did it. Mick was right. It was all on computers.

After the tour, we checked out the parking lot in back. There was a back door that led into the spa, for customers. And there was a utility door at the side, which led to an alley.

"I guess Kristle would stake out the place from the front. Then she could move back here and wait for Deva to come out to her car," Mick said.

"Hold on," I said. "Deva wouldn't drive herself. She'd have a car from the studio pick her up and fetch her, or wait outside the spa. What are we going to do about that? Hire a limousine? This is hopeless." I slumped against a Mercedes hood, and the car alarm went off with a deafening electronic beep.

Mick and I bolted like jackrabbits. We ran down the alley to the front, where we collapsed against the bug, laughing. It felt good to laugh, even if it was only for a few seconds.

"So, Mr. Big Shot," I said. "Where are you going to get a limo?"

But Mick just swept back his hair and grinned.

"Don't tell me," I groaned. "Leave it to you, Beaver."

19//makeover

Mick's next-door neighbor turned out to work for the local funeral parlor. In addition to driving hearses, he had also bought his own limo to drive family members to funerals. Mick traded him ten free guitar lessons for loaning us his limo three nights that week.

I sat in Mick's living room, waiting while he made the deal. It isn't like any home I've ever been in. Mick and his mom live in downtown Mohawk Falls, for one thing. It's mostly a business section, and it isn't exactly thriving. Everyone shops at the surrounding malls, where there is plenty of parking and all the stores are familiar because they're in every town in America.

The mayor talks a lot about "reclaiming our fine heritage," but downtown is

still pretty seedy. A bunch of the old buildings have been renovated, and there are a
couple of hip coffee shops and restaurants
and furniture stores, but not many people
live there. As a matter of fact, I didn't
think anyone did, until Mick brought me
there.

He'd parked the car in an alley and led
me up the outdoor back staircase of a ram-
bling old house. "It used to be a rooming
house," he explained. He and his mom have
a three-bedroom apartment on the top floor.
The ceiling slopes, but it's pretty high. And
out the windows you can see the whole valley spread out.

The furniture looks like thrift store finds
that have been painted and re-covered. It's
cheerful and bright, and I can imagine it's
cozy on a cold winter's night.

"Cozy?" Mick scoffed when I mentioned
this. "Try freezing." He dragged an old
wooden chair that had been painted
turquoise into the middle of the kitchen
floor. Then he placed newspapers all
around it.

I eyed it nervously. "What's going on?"

Grinning, Mick flourished a pair of scissors at me. "Velcome to ze salon of dreams," he said.

I shook my head. "No way."

"Come on," Mick said. "You need a new look."

"Gee, thanks."

His smile faded. "For Camille?"

I blew out a breath. "For Camille."

Nervously, I sat in the chair. Mick circled me, staring at my hair. I was secretly very proud of it. It was long and thick, and I wailed if my mom trimmed more than an inch off it. It was hot in the summer, and it was a pain to wash it and dry it, but I'd never wanted to cut it.

"Can't I just wear a wig?" I asked.

"Cheap wigs are obvious," Mick said, making the first cut.

I saw the first curl hit the floor. I wanted to cry. "How about a hat?"

"Just trust me, okay?" Another long tendril hit the newspaper.

I laced my fingers together tightly, closed my eyes, and listened to the *snip snip* of the scissors.

Mick was halfway through the haircut when we heard the door slam.

"I'm home!"

"In here!" Mick yelled.

A moment later, his mom stood in the doorway. I started to say hello, but her mouth fell open, and a look of horror came over her face.

"Oh, my—"

"What is it?" I asked fearfully.

"Give me those scissors," his mom rapped out to Mick. She patted my shoulder. "Now, don't you worry, sweetie. I'll fix you right up."

"I was trying to give Mina a Deva Winter cut. It looks easy when you do it," Mick said to his mom. "I just thought I had to cut it short."

"That's great, if you want Mina to look like a marine," his mother said sweetly.

I bolted off the chair. "A what?"

Mick's mom put her hand on my shoulder and gently guided me back. "Don't worry, sweetie. I'm a haircutter. I can fix any disaster."

"You mean it's . . . a *disaster*?" I asked, my voice wobbling. "Can I see it?"

She sighed. "I wouldn't, if I were you, hon. You're a nice kid, and I want you to stay friends with Mick. First of all, we need to shampoo your hair." She looked at Mick. "If you cut it dry like that, Mina is going to look like Ronald McDonald."

I shot Mick a black look.

"At least you'd get free cheeseburgers," Mick said helpfully.

Mrs. Mahoney groaned. "Come on, Mina. Time to hit the kitchen sink."

Mick's mom shampooed my hair in a delicious-smelling shampoo and wrapped it in a towel. She combed it out slowly, easing through the tangles. Then she sat me back down in the kitchen chair and studied my face. By the time she made the first cut with the scissors, I knew I was in the hands of a pro. Humming, she snipped here and there. Tendril after tendril hit the floor. My neck felt suddenly cool, and my head felt light.

Finally, she stepped back and nodded. "Okay. Done."

She led me to the mirror in the bathroom. I let out a gasp when I saw myself. "My hair!" I touched the ends, which now wisped around my ears. "It's gone."

"You look fabulous," Mick's mother said firmly.

I looked again. "I have cheekbones," I said wonderingly.

"And look at your eyes—you have beautiful eyes. You look gorgeous." Mrs. Mahoney stared in the mirror at me. "Doesn't she, Mick?"

Mick lurked in the doorway to the bathroom. I turned, excited at my new look. But Mick just looked at his feet. "She looks okay."

Mrs. Mahoney rolled her eyes. "Teenage guys. The worst."

"You said it," I said, and we giggled together.

"Well, I don't look like Deva Winter," I said. "But I do have her hair."

"Why do you want to look like Deva?" his mom asked.

"Uh, we're having this celebrity look-alike day at school," Mick said, improvising.

I looked down at my clothes. I was wearing jeans, but they weren't *cool* jeans. They were just my usual faded straight-legs. And my oxford button-down shirt wasn't exactly cutting edge. Not to mention my canvas sneakers.

"You need a little help, hon," Mick's mom said tactfully. "I think it's time to raid my closet."

In only thirty minutes, I was a completely different person. My hair was moussed, and I was wearing red lipstick, and eyeliner. Mick's mom was about my size, and I was wearing her black jeans and clunky-heeled boots. After trying about twenty different tops, we finally decided on a regular plain white T-shirt of Mick's. Mrs. Mahoney added a red chiffon scarf tied around my neck. Then I slipped into a black leather jacket.

"Perfect!" Mrs. Mahoney beamed. "The ultimate Hollywood actress look."

I looked in the mirror. I still looked like me, only a hipper version. But maybe coming out of a limo, with sunglasses on, I just might pass.

I couldn't believe what I saw in the mirror. I had made the cool jump!

We all congratulated ourselves, and Mrs. Mahoney went off humming into the kitchen to make herself some tea.

Mick and I just looked at each other. The afternoon had been totally fun. But now it was time to get serious.

I called the spa and pretended to be Jennifer, which basically meant that I was rude. I said I wanted five o'clock appointments for Deva every day that week.

No problem.

Then, a few hours later, I called and made an appointment under my own name at the same time.

They'd "squeeze me in."

The next day, everything was set. Mick not only borrowed the limo, he borrowed a uniform. He borrowed cellular phones, and we put each other's numbers on speed dial.

We drove to Saratoga Springs. I sat up front to keep Mick company, but as soon as we reached the outskirts I slipped into the back. When we got to the spa, I put on my cool shades and the leather jacket. I leaped from the car and hurried into the building, carefully keeping my face away from the street.

I had a manicure, and then a "skin technician" rubbed a mud mask on my skin. It was goopy and smelled like a swamp, but after she rinsed it off, my skin glowed. You never know what a little marsh muck can do for you.

I lingered in the big locker room. I flipped through magazines in the lounge. I waited for Mick to ring me to tell me that Kristle was outside, staking me out. But nothing happened. I left at dusk, walking quickly down the stairs—*Don't look around!* Mick had ordered me. *Stars never do!*—and sliding into the backseat of the limo.

"See anything?" Mick asked.

"Zip," I said. "But my skin looks terrific."

He started the car with a sigh. "We'll try again tomorrow."

But Kristle didn't show up on the second afternoon, either. I had a really incredible herbal mineral soak that the attendant assured me would "remove all those nasty toxins." I was using my pitiful savings account money to bankroll this ambush, and all those birthday checks from my grandmother were disappearing into mud and seaweed. The spa was going to bankrupt me, but at least my pores would be clean.

On my third visit, I opted for a private steam room. I padded toward the room in my terry cloth robe. The cell phone was in my pocket, and I was afraid the steam would ruin it, so I hung the robe right outside the door. I grabbed a couple of the fluffy white towels that seemed to be stacked everywhere. I couldn't imagine their laundry bill.

It was my first experience with a steam room. I felt as though I couldn't breathe, but after a few minutes, I got used to it. I stretched out on one of the redwood benches and closed my eyes. I tented the towel over my face to create a mini-facial. I was beginning to see why stars look so gorgeous all the time. It's because they're pampered. This spa is like an auto detail shop. Every part of me got shined and buffed, vacuumed, and sandblasted. Pretty soon, even *I* would be gorgeous.

Mick had told me over and over again that I'd be safe in the spa. He didn't think Kristle would try to go inside, but he was watching the entrances in both the front and the alley. For the first time, I relaxed. The steam felt so good. And the spa was busy with all kinds of workers and clients. Kristle would have to be crazy to try to approach Deva here.

She'd have to be crazy. . . .

A trickle of unease slid down my spine. Or was it sweat?

Wait a second. She is crazy!

Just then, I heard the door open softly, then close. The steam was so thick, I could only make out a white blur. The figure tossed some water on the special "wellness lava rocks with herbal notes." More steam rose.

The voice was hushed, polite. "Deva?"

Relax. It's just a spa technician who thinks I'm Deva. She wants to make sure my toxins are draining.

Underneath the towel, I squinted across the room. A plump figure dressed in a too-tight suit took a step toward me.

"It's me," Ronnie Harbin said. "I just had to talk to you."

I froze. *Ronnie. The stalker was Ronnie!* It wasn't K. D. at all—the initials had been a coincidence. Kristle Pollack had changed her name. Why didn't we think of Ronnie as a suspect? She was so devoted to Deva. Her number one fan. . . .

Stay calm, I told myself. I kept the towel on my head like a hood, shading my face. *Slowly*, I swung my legs to the floor. I had to get to that phone! I inched a bit closer to the door.

"Don't be scared," Ronnie said. "I mean, I can't believe I'm doing this. I totally respect your privacy. But I never thought you'd actually come to where I live! I couldn't not meet you. I've been trying and trying. I've been waiting at the movie set."

I moved another fraction toward the door.

"You have no idea what a big fan I am," Ronnie said.

I sprang off the seat and rushed at the door.

"Deva, wait—"

Ronnie grabbed my arm, but I was able to break her grip. She stumbled backward as the towel fell off my head.

"Hey, you're not Deva! You're"—Ronnie's brown eyes grew wider—"that girl—"

I pushed her hard. She fell back onto the redwood bench. I fumbled with the door handle and pushed it open. The cool air was a relief.

I threw my weight against the door, holding it closed. It shuddered as Ronnie pounded on it. I kept it closed with all my weight while I looked around for something to brace it with.

Someone had left an umbrella leaning against a locker. I was just able to keep my weight against the door while I hooked the umbrella with my bare toes. I dragged it toward me.

"Let me out! Let me out!" Ronnie thumped against the door again. For a big girl, she wasn't very strong.

Quickly, I slipped the umbrella through the door handle. It was one of those huge, sturdy, expensive umbrellas. It would hold until Mick got there.

I reached for my robe and slipped into it as I grabbed the phone. I pressed speed dial, and Mick came on immediately.

"I'm here."

"It's Ronnie, Mick," I gasped. "Ronnie! She's in the steam room! Quick! I've got her!"

"I'm there," Mick yelled, and broke the connection.

I put my mouth near the crack of the door. "Relax, Ronnie!" I yelled. "This will only take a minute. Enjoy the steam!"

The door to the locker room *whooshed* open. Out of the corner of my eye, I saw one of the white-jacketed spa technicians.

Keeping my eye on the door, I said, "Thank goodness. I know this looks weird, but I have a major criminal trapped in your steam room."

Suddenly, my arm was yanked behind me. It was twisted up behind my back, making me cry out. My eyes stung with tears from the pain.

"You think so?" The voice hissed in my ear.

Then I was spun around and slammed against the locker room wall. My head smashed against the tile, making my teeth snap together. I bit my tongue and tasted blood in my mouth.

K. D.—Kristle—stared at me. Her mouth was twisted in an angry grimace.

"Hey, what's going on?" I asked, trying to bluff. *Where was Mick?* "I was just—"

"Shut up." She slammed my head against the wall again. "Let's go."

My head rang, and pain shot through me again as Kristle yanked my arm behind me. I couldn't believe how strong she was. She stuffed a washcloth in my mouth, then tied a robe sash around that. She kept my wrists in the grip of one powerful hand. Then she pushed me toward the door to the corridor.

Mick! Hurry! my mind screamed.

Kristle looked down the empty corridor, then yanked me across the hall and into another room. It was a linen storage closet, narrow and long, running alongside the corridor. It was lined with shelves filled with sheets and towels and folded terry cloth robes.

She pushed me against the wall. I could

smell her perspiration. She stared at me with sudden recognition.

"Wait. I know you. I know you—"

I shook my head vigorously.

"Yeah, I do. I know *exactly* who you are." On the word "exactly," she slammed me back against the wall. "You're Camille's friend. From the mall. What's going on? Where's Deva? I saw her come in."

I shook my head. It hurt to shake it.

Kristle held me by the hair, thinking. "Wait. I'm getting this. It was you. You. You wanted me to think it was her. You came out of a limousine!"

I shook my head again. Kristle yanked my arm behind my back and twisted it. It felt as though it was going to pop out of its socket.

"Let's go for a ride," she said.

She forced me to walk. I tried to stumble in order to slow her down, but every time I did, she yanked me back up. The pain was sending spots dancing in front of my eyes. I tried to knock things down as we walked, hoping to make noise. Piles of towels and robes tumbled to the floor. The soft terry didn't make a sound. But at least I was leaving a trail.

Kristle reached the door at the end of the narrow room. She shoved it open with a hip. I realized that it was the laundry delivery entrance that looked out on the alley at the side of the building.

And Mick was probably right now releasing Ronnie from the steam room, not believing her story, thinking it was a bluff. He would be wondering where I was.

Look for me, Mick. Now.

It was dark in the alley. While Kristle checked both ways to make sure it was deserted, I was able to deliberately lose my balance and fall. My knee scraped against the concrete. But Kristle's grip stayed firm. She roughly hauled me back up again.

I kept working my mouth, trying to dislodge the gag. I felt as though I would choke, or swallow the washcloth. I kept pushing against it, trying to work my tongue around it. With all my struggling, the sash was coming free. I could feel it loosening. I didn't have much time!

Kristle dragged me the rest of the way to

her car, a dark brown compact. She kept both of my wrists in her grip while she slid the key into the lock of the trunk. But when she tried to open it, I managed to twist away for an instant.

I tore the sash away and spit out the washcloth. I screamed.

Kristle kneed me in the stomach with casual viciousness, her intent expression never changing.

I fell, gasping, holding on to the fender. Kristle grabbed my wrist and twisted it so hard that searing white pain flashed through me. I wondered if she'd just broken it.

Kristle picked me up as though I were a doll. She threw me in the trunk. My breath had left me, and I couldn't scream. I tried to kick her.

And then the alley door burst open, and Mick ran out. He took in the scene immediately and began to charge.

Kristle pushed me back, making my wrist scream in pain when it hit the spare tire. The trunk lid slammed down, and I was in darkness.

I heard the *thunk* of a car door, the *vroom* of the engine, Mick shouting, the *thump* of something hitting the car.

Tires squealed. The car accelerated. I heard the steady *whir* of tires on pavement. After long minutes, the car slowed to a normal speed.

And I knew that Kristle had gotten away.

21//don't panic

I didn't know what scared me more. The pain, or the thought of what was to come.

I struggled not to panic. I couldn't move very much. The spare tire nudged my hip. I felt around for a jack with my good hand, but the trunk was empty.

What could I do? It was dark now. Mick was no expert at tailing someone—would he be able to follow Kristle? Although every bump we went over sent my head into the trunk roof, making me feel as though we were speeding, I had a feeling we weren't. That meant Kristle wasn't being followed. Or she didn't *think* she was. She probably didn't want to attract attention. I wished she would speed—maybe she'd get pulled over. Then I could pound on the trunk and scream.

But she wouldn't let that happen.

Is this how she'd kidnapped Camille? Had Camille lain in this trunk, too? Had she been in pain, and afraid, but still not able to believe it was really happening?

But I had an advantage over Camille. I knew what Kristle was capable of. That meant I had to risk everything to get away.

Camille, were you this scared?

The car wheeled around the corner. My wrist sent another shock of pain up my arm as it pressed against the tire. How would Mick's big, lumbering limo be able to keep up with Kristle's nimble car? He'd have to hang way back so she wouldn't spot him. He'd have to keep her in sight without giving himself away.

Camille, help me.

The ride was smoother now, and faster. The highway. Was Mick tailing us?

Tail . . .

I had an inspiration. Carefully, I slid forward as much as I could. I reached out and felt along the trunk until I reached the left taillight. I yanked on the wires.

With one taillight out, it would make the

car easier to follow. And maybe Kristle would get pulled over by a cop. If I was lucky.

It was the only thing I could do. I cradled my wrist. It was already starting to swell. I tried to brace myself against the bumps. And I tried not to wonder if I could run out of air.

The speed of the car decreased, and we stopped and started a few times. We must have left the freeway. After a few minutes, the road got bumpy. My head kept knocking against the roof.

What advantage did I have? I was bruised and in pain, and my wrist could be broken. Kristle was amazingly strong. I couldn't fight her.

But I could surprise her.

I didn't have a weapon, but I did have my feet. I wished I was wearing shoes. I'd just have to try to kick her in the face. Or maybe I could use my good hand to lunge at her eyes. Could I lunge at a person's eyes?

I thought of Camille. Yes, I could.

The car slowed down. We went down a hill. We bumped along slowly. I heard the sound of rocks being kicked up by the tires. Then we rolled to a stop.

I braced myself. I was ready to fling myself out at Kristle as soon as the trunk lid popped.

I heard a *click,* and the lid rose a few inches. I waited.

Nothing.

I waited another few minutes. Then I pushed at it cautiously. No one was there.

I crawled out of the trunk, wincing at the pain of my wrist, keeping it against my body. I smelled something familiar in the air. The river. I was near the river. I knew right where I was now. There were two abandoned factories outside of Mohawk Falls. One had made toys, and the other had been a textile factory. Their dark, hulking shapes loomed against the night.

I knew now where Camille had been held. But hadn't the police and the FBI searched the factories? I was sure that they had.

I hardly felt the rough, pointed stones on my bare feet. I peered around the car to the driver's side. No Kristle. What was going on?

As I started to turn back, I caught the flash of something moving toward me. I felt the blow at the back of my head, and then points of light exploded behind my eyes.

Dark. Musty. Hard. Cold. And then—
breath hissing out from my teeth when I
moved—pain.

White pain that grew and pounded in my
skull. I breathed in and out, slowly. It less-
ened, just a bit, but it felt like sweet relief.

I counted ten slow breaths. My head
started to clear. I realized there were ropes
tying my ankles together. My wrists were
tied to a leg of something. A table? My fin-
gertips brushed against something cold.
Metal.

Just flexing my fingers brought fresh pain
from my wrist. I moaned.

"You're finally awake. Jeez."

The voice came out of the darkness. I
peered ahead of me, but I only saw black.

"I didn't want to hurt you," Kristle said.

"You shouldn't have tried to get away. You shouldn't have tried to trick me."

My words came out of a dry mouth. I realized I was horribly thirsty. "I'm sorry," I croaked.

"No, you're not. We're not friends yet. When we're friends, you'll be sorry. I can wait."

She sounded so . . . calm. So calm, and so crazy.

"Camille," I forced out. My head was pounding.

"She was here, too," Kristle said. "Yeah. She was really pretty. Prettier than you. But she wasn't very nice to me, you know. I thought she'd be nice, like Deva. When I offered her a ride at the mall, she took it. She came back to find you, I think, but you'd left. I said I just got off, and did she need a ride? I could tell she thought I was a nerd. A geek. A loser. I'm not stupid. But she said okay because she hated taking the bus. And so I started driving, and I didn't take her where she wanted to go, and she got mad. But she couldn't get out of the car. She thought I was going to rob her or something.

I could tell she was a little scared. I brought her here, and she started running away, so I had to hit her with the shovel, like I hit you. Does it hurt?"

"It hurts," I said. "Water?"

"Oh. Yeah. Okay." The darkness shaped itself into a form. Kristle moved toward me. She held near my face one of those bottles that runners use, and I sucked at the long plastic straw. Cool water ran down my throat.

"Thanks," I said.

"You're welcome. Anyway, like I said, the whole thing with Camille was disappointing because I could tell she was only pretending to be my friend. What's your name?" Kristle asked suddenly.

"Mina," I said.

"That's a weird name."

"It's short for Wilhelmina," I said. "My great-aunt."

"I kind of like it. I like old-fashioned names. I hate trendy names. Everybody's Ashley and Heather now. My mother is an idiot. She gave me such a stupid name. Kristle Daisy."

"Your mother," I forced out, "misses you, Kristle."

"K. D.! My name is K. D.! And how do you know my mother?"

"I met her," I said. "I went to your house. I wanted to . . . to get to know you better. I saw your scrapbooks."

"They're stupid." I heard a rhythmic thumping, as though Kristle was hitting the floor with her fist. "Stupid, stupid, stupid."

"But you won so many times," I said. "And you were so pretty."

"*Were* pretty. *Were* pretty," Kristle rapped out. "Then I grew up. All of a sudden, people didn't say how pretty I was anymore. Did you know that Deva was a child model? She grew up pretty, though. But I think we have that in common. Because it's hard, not really having a real childhood. You're always trying to please adults, and you never really make friends. You get used to trying to look cute. I never had friends. I just had my mom."

Kristle's voice changed. It became syrupy, sweet, and singsong. "We have each other, Krissie. Just you and me, kid. What do we need anybody else for? Give me a kiss. Give me a hug. Give me a smile. Give me that twinkle, little star. All I have is you. All you have is me. You have to take care of us. Keep dancing. You have to practice. You have to be the best. I know it's late, you brat, but *keep dancing!*"

"She said she misses you," I said.

"I don't want to talk about my mother, okay?" Kristle said mildly. "If you want to be friends, just don't talk about her. The happiest day of my life was when I left. I was even homeless, and I didn't care. In L.A. I lived on the street. Then I started hanging around this gym, and I started bodybuilding. It was so cool. I was really good at it. The trainer gave me some steroids. I am really strong."

"I know," I said.

She laughed. "Yeah, I guess you do. I won some championships, okay? So I called Mom and told her, and she said, oh, that's so *unfeminine*. She didn't even congratulate me. So then I thought, I can be a bodyguard to a star. That's something I can be really, really good at. So I picked my favorite actress. But they wouldn't hire me. Deva never even saw me. Her 'people' wouldn't let her. I just know if she met me, she'd like me! Stars get to be friends with their body-guards, you know."

"Sometimes," I said. My arms were start-ing to ache badly. It was hard because they were twisted to one side, and I couldn't stretch my body.

"All the time! I could protect Deva. I didn't kill Camille, you know." Kristle's voice was low. "I promise."

"What happened?" I asked.

"She tried to get away and she really conked herself on the head. There's a lot of dangerous stuff around here. I think she went crazy because the police were here, searching, and they didn't find us. Do you know about Prohibition?"

Her topics were swinging so crazily. It took a minute for me to understand the question. "Yes," I said. "Kind of. When it was illegal to sell liquor. In the nineteen twenties."

"Right. It used to come down from Canada. They'd load it on ships right here and float it down to New York City. I think this factory owner was a bootlegger. That's what they called them."

"Camille . . . , " I said, wanting her to return to the topic.

"Right. Well. So, she landed on her head and got a huge gash. It bled a lot. She asked me to take her to the hospital."

I started to cry. I bit my lip so that I wouldn't sob out loud. I wished I could put my hands over my ears. I didn't want to hear this. Couldn't hear it. Couldn't picture Camille, hurt, begging. . . .

"I said I would. And I meant it! But I had to figure out a plan, first. I mean, what if Deva found out that I let Camille get hurt while I was watching her? I couldn't let that happen. I didn't realize it was serious, what had happened. Hey, I'm not a nurse!"

The tears ran into the corners of my mouth, down my chin, dripped on my robe.

"I went in, and she'd stopped breathing. I knew she was dead. Her body was cold. I was so mad! I yelled at her. That sounds crazy, and I don't want to sound crazy, because I'm not. But, listen, anybody would go a little nuts if that happened to them, right?"

I didn't answer.

"Right?"

"Right," I choked out.

"So I took her to the river. I was hoping they wouldn't find her. It was a dark, dark night." Kristle's voice became hypnotic. "The river was like thick, black oil. It was beautiful. I could smell it and taste it in the air. I put rocks in her pockets. I said a prayer. And I just let the current take her. I think it would be a lovely way to be buried, don't you? Fish nibbling on your toes while you swim down this long, long green river."

She was quiet. I leaned my head back against the cold metal of the machine I was tethered to. I pressed my cheek against it.

"So you see I'm not crazy, right?" Kristle asked.

"Yes," I said.

"You're still lying."

Talk to her. Convince her you're her friend. Be smarter. Talk to her.

Because if Mick had been able to follow us, he'd be here by now. It was all up to me.

"I was friends with Camille all through grammar school," I said. "Best friends. We both were different looking. Camille was overweight."

"Really?" Kristle sounded interested.

"Really. She liked sweets. Her parents got divorced, and I guess she ate for comfort, you know? And I was really, really skinny. Too skinny. And my hair was frizzy and long. But we didn't care, because we had each other."

"That's nice," Kristle said. "Friends are nice."

"Then last summer, Camille went to the shore with her mom," I said. My head was pounding, but I tried to concentrate, tried to find the right words. "She got a haircut and lost weight, and bought new clothes. She even got a boyfriend. And when she came back to school, she was different. And we weren't friends anymore."

"You mean she just dropped you?" Kristle asked.

"Just about," I said. "She met new friends. The cool crowd, you know? And she started dating all these guys."

"That's awful!" Kristle said. "You know, I never liked her."

"So you see," I said, "I know what being lonely is like."

"Oh," Kristle said. "It's hard, right?"

"It's very hard," I said. "That's why I think we could be friends."

"Did you ever do anything mean?" Kristle asked in a low tone.

"In social studies last fall, we were supposed to pick partners for a project," I said. "This was before Camille really dropped me. But she was getting friendly with this girl, Gigi, who's the coolest of the cool. Anyway, Camille and I were always partners if we had to do projects or whatever. But this time, she didn't even look at me. She looked at Gigi. And the two of them nodded, and smiled, and I didn't know who I hated more, Gigi or Camille. After class, Camille told me that she chose Gigi because they had the same interests. Like Camille had any interest in social studies, or like Gigi had a brain at all. Give me a break. So the day they were supposed to make their presentation, I opened

Camille's locker—I still knew her combination. And I stole the tape out of the cassette player that she was going to use for her presentation. I thought Gigi would blame Camille for forgetting it, and they'd get into a huge fight."

"What happened?" Kristle breathed.

"Gigi didn't care. She just laughed and called Camille an airhead, and Camille laughed and said they'd probably get a D, anyway. And I knew that I'd done it for nothing."

"So you know what it's like, to want to do bad things if people don't love you," Kristle said.

"I do, Kristle," I said. "Everybody does. Everybody knows how hard it is. That's why, if you let me go, everyone will understand why you did what you did."

Kristle's voice was muffled. "I don't think so."

"I'll *help* them understand," I said. "I'll talk for you. We'll face everyone together."

"That's a nice thought."

There was a rustling movement. Kristle crawled toward me. She came close, close enough so that I could feel her breath on my face. It was as scary as a bear's.

"I'm really sorry, Mina. I really am. But don't you see? I can't ever let you go."

23//desperate measures

Okay. I was scared. And in pain. Part of me felt every grain of dust on the floorboards, and part of me felt as if I were floating above myself, watching.

But my brain was working. Maybe better than it ever had in my whole life. Because it wasn't me straining my brain, trying to remember a fact, or a logarithm. It was me *knowing* something, making leaps from fact to fact.

Like this: Kristle attacked when she was frightened or cornered, or betrayed. But she would find it hard to actually kill in cold blood.

So my best chance was to keep Kristle talking. Or try to get Kristle to leave, so that I'd have a chance to see if there was any possible way to escape.

Camille had tried. Maybe there was some way.

Dust floated up and tickled my nose. I knew that if I sneezed, my head would feel as though it were about to explode. So I closed my eyes, trying to suppress the urge.

So much dust, and mildew. I could smell it. It was like every crummy cabin you ever smelled, with a big fan blowing the mildew in your face. We used to rent a cabin by a lake in Maine, and my brother Doug always has a hard time. He has asthma.

And, just then, the idea floated into my brain, and I tested it. Maybe it could work. I know the sound of struggling lungs. I could fake a wheeze. I used to imitate Doug, to make fun of him, before Mom told me to cut it out.

Don't think about home.

I started with a raspy breath. Then I faked a wheeze. Another one, bigger this time.

"Hey . . . , " Kristle said.

Another wheeze.

"What's wrong with you?"

"I'm . . . allergic," I wheezed out, "to dust."

"I swept!" Kristle cried.

I went into full-wheeze mode. I hoped that Kristle didn't know anyone with asthma, because I sounded pretty pathetic.

But she was buying it. "Can't you relax? You're probably making it worse." She sounded nervous.

"I . . . can't," I said. "Need my inhaler. Back at the spa."

"I'm not going back there!" Kristle cried. "No way!"

"There's over-the-counter stuff," I wheezed. "Medication I can take. Please? Any drugstore."

"No way." But she sounded uncertain now.

Every rattling breath I took made my head pound. I gritted my teeth against the pain. I felt as though I might faint. I couldn't keep this up. Couldn't. But I had to. . . .

"Cut it out! You're driving me nuts! Just be quiet!" Kristle said nervously.

But a moment later, over the sound of my breathing, I heard a shuffling noise. Kristle was retreating.

My eyes strained through the darkness. I

couldn't see anything. Then I heard a creak.

At last, I could see the door. There must have been moonlight flooding the room next to this one, because suddenly, I could make out outlines and shapes. I saw Kristle slip through an opening and close it behind her. There wasn't even a crack of light. I was plunged into darkness again.

My hands were tied around the leg of some kind of machine, but I could slide my wrists up and down and feel along the leg. I explored the floor with my bare toes. The floor was wood, and uneven, with deep grooves running down it. Probably from moving equipment around, I guessed.

Then my toes hit something cool and smooth. I maneuvered my feet around it and tried to pick it up, but it clattered back onto the floor. Finally, straining, I captured it between two of my toes. I slid it up toward me. I was able to lift my foot and bring it up to my good hand.

It was a hair clip. Camille's! She'd been wearing it that day. It was metal, with a painted design on the front. The tip of the clasp pricked my finger. I tested it. Sharp.

Camille had sharpened it somehow! Maybe against the metal of the machine.

This time, I slid my wrists up as high as they would go, ignoring the pain that shot down my arm. I reached some kind of joint. It was loose, and I could wiggle it. I strained to see through the darkness and feel with my fingers. Two screws were missing.

Camille had used the clip as a screwdriver, I guessed. She'd been able to get the screws loose. Now I could see the faint scratches where the paint had been worn away from the metal. And once, there had been a part that braced the leg against the machine. Camille had probably unscrewed it. I could see its partner, still screwed to the machine. There were teeth on one side of it where they fit into a gear. Maybe Camille had tried to use it as a weapon. Maybe that's what she had fallen on. The end was sharp and could have punctured someone easily.

The other brace would take hours to get loose, I saw. But the gear now only had one screw holding it to the machine.

Using Camille's clip, I scraped and twisted,

working at the screw. It seemed to take hours, because every few minutes I had to slide my wrists down and rest. My arms were aching. But I knew I didn't have much time.

At last, I felt the screw give. Working quickly now, forgetting the pain, I unscrewed it from the gear. It was easy to use my good hand to slip the gear off its mounting. It fell onto my lap.

It was rusty, but the spikes were fairly sharp. I worked at the rope binding my wrists. It began to fray. It was working!

I sawed through one rope and untangled myself from the knot. But as I reached down for my ankles, I heard the creak of the door.

I slumped over, my head on my chest. My heart was beating so loudly that I was sure Kristle could hear it. But I held my breath.

"Mina? Mina?" Kristle tiptoed toward me. "I got you some spray junk. Hey. You must feel better. I can't hear you breathe."

Something whistled through the air and hit me on the forehead. I didn't flinch. It fell in my lap. It was an inhaler.

"Mina? Don't play games like that. I don't trust you. Mina?"

Kristle crept closer. Between my fingers was the small, sharp gear, spikes outward. I let out air slowly through my nose, took another silent breath.

Kristle was inches away now. I sprang forward, the gear clenched in my fist, spikes outward, and punched her in the face. Then I kicked her ankles from underneath her. Roaring with anger and pain, Kristle went down.

I scrabbled at the ropes on my ankles. Within seconds I was free. And I ran.

24//the longest fall

"Mean!" Kristle howled. "So mean!"

I ran blindly, my hands in front of my face. I didn't feel pain anymore; I didn't even feel fear. I ran right into a wall, bounced off, and kept on running. But there was no doorknob that I could see.

Behind me, I could hear Kristle getting to her feet.

"I'm bleeding!" she cried in a wounded voice. "I'm really bleeding, Mina! I can't see!"

Kristle was angry now. And that meant she could hurt me. All bets were off.

I felt along the wall. A hint of something—cooler air—alerted me to a crack. The door was flush against the wall. It was hidden! The memory of Kristle talking about Prohibition flashed through my mind.

I was in a secret room. No wonder the police hadn't found Camille!

But there was a way out, because Kristle had found it. My fingers ran along the crack, following it.

Kristle got to her feet and yowled. "My ankle! I twisted it! It hurts! You can't get out, so don't bother." She groaned.

I found it. A piece of wood moved beneath my fingers, and I swung it back. There was a latch! I yanked it, and the door moved. I pulled, and it swung toward me. I only had to open it a few inches. I wiggled through.

"Hey!" Kristle screamed.

I ran through a large empty room. Trash was piled in a few corners, hunks of machinery that had rusted long ago. The windows were caked with dirt, but there was light enough to see. The river was on my right, which meant that I was running toward the front of the building. I should be able to find an entrance, or at least a broken window to crawl through.

Kristle was moving slowly because of her twisted ankle. But she knew where she was going, and I didn't. I told myself not to look back, that it would only slow me down.

Then I saw it—a door in the corner. A piece of wood was shoved through the handle so that no one could push it in from outside. But it was easy to slip out the wood and pull open the door.

The air was cool, and I could smell the river as I ran from the factory. But where could I go? These roads were deserted at night. Town was far away. Kristle could hunt me down in minutes.

The river. There was a dam on the river with a lock so that boats could navigate down to the Hudson. Someone would probably be there, a security guard, at least. It was my best bet. And if no one was there, I knew there was thick vegetation along the river's edge. It would be easier to hide from Kristle there.

Slipping and sliding, I made my way down the hill, then across an old railroad track toward the embankment. I could hear Kristle crashing down the hill behind me. I scrambled up the embankment toward the dam. Up here, I could see the sloping concrete of the dam, and the water-fall cascading into the dark river.

Hooking my fingers onto the Cyclone fence, I stood on the concrete walkway, looking down into the canal that had been built to allow ship traffic down the river, avoiding the waterfall. The locks were below me. If I climbed the fence to the other side, I could edge along the lip of the walk-way and get to the building that controlled the dam. It was risky. But I had no choice.

I climbed the fence and swung myself over. I scrambled down, carefully feeling for the ledge with my feet. I landed, holding on to the fence. Going as fast as I dared, I started moving toward the building. I prayed that Kristle would spend time searching the bushes along the river. If I was lucky, she wouldn't see me.

But I wasn't lucky. Suddenly, Kristle rose out from the darkness, making me gasp. With a snarl, she hurled herself against the fence. It shuddered, and panic shot through me as I swayed over the concrete and dark water below.

My fingers were slick with sweat as I

reached for another grip. Kristle hurled herself against the fence again. It shimmied, and I felt myself tipping back over the abyss. Every muscle strained as I concentrated on holding on.

Kristle was sobbing now, deep, wrenching sobs that erupted into howls as she hit against the fence. I prayed it would hold. I kept moving, trying to time my grips on the fence against her assaults.

Then, Kristle began to scale the fence. It bent underneath our weight. I looked down at the machinery below, the huge sluices and the metal gates, and the cold, black water. Then I snapped my gaze back up.

The trick is not to look down. Don't look back. Don't look down. Keep moving.

I kept moving. Kristle was halfway up the fence now. She was close to me. I could almost reach out and touch her.

And then, over the noise of the waterfall, I heard someone call.

"Kristle!"

Kristle and I both froze. We peered down at the embankment. A dark form was racing up it. Mick!

"Kristle!" he shouted, moving fast, not stopping. "Don't! I have a message for you."

She clung to the wire fence. Blood was smeared on her cheek from where I'd hit her. I'd cut her near her eye.

"It's from Deva!" Mick shouted.

Kristle plastered herself against the fence. Her fingers curled into the openings, and her cheek pressed against the metal. She was shaking.

"You're lying," she whispered.

But Mick couldn't hear her over the sound of the water. He was on the concrete ledge now, walking toward her. He held out his hands, palms toward her, as if to say he wouldn't hurt her.

"Don't come any closer!" she screamed.

Mick stopped. "I went to talk to her," he said. "She wants to see you. She knows everything, Kristle—how much you want to be her friend. She knows that things went wrong. She wants to help."

"You're lying," Kristle sobbed.

Mick looked at me. He nodded, as if to say *everything is okay now.* It made me feel better, even though it wasn't true. At least I wasn't alone.

"Come on, Kristle," Mick said gently. "You don't want to hurt Mina. And Deva's waiting in the car."

"She's not!" Kristle cried. Tears ran down her face. "She never comes! And I"—she took a deep, shuddering breath, and her mouth opened in a huge, strained O as she howled a sob—"I . . . tried . . . so hard!"

"Kristle." Mick's voice was calm. "Come on. Come with me. We can talk. All of us. We want to talk."

Kristle turned to me. Through the triangles of the metal fence, her eyes met mine. Her gaze was unnerving, suddenly blank, the gaze of a shark.

Moonlight glittered on her tears. "You're so mean," she whispered to me, but her gaze wandered past my shoulder, to the lights across the river. "Everyone is just . . . so . . . mean."

With one powerful motion of her arms, she swung herself to the top of the fence. She balanced for just a moment at the top.

Then she simply took a giant step out into space.

I screamed and pressed against the fence. I heard her body hit the concrete. And then, long seconds later, I heard the splash.

//epilogue

Retrieve: a:///life.
(Journal of Mina Sterling Kurtz)

They found her body floating below. I was in the ambulance, so I didn't see it. Neither did Mick. He was sitting with me, holding a blanket around my shoulders. It kept slipping off.

But when I dream about it—and I dream about it every night—I see her body. I'm there as they pluck her out of the river. In my dream, they cradle her like a baby. Sometimes, I'm the one who cradles her.

Which is seriously strange, because she killed my best friend. And she would have killed me if she could. I think. Sometimes, I'm not sure.

My parents are talking about a shrink. But I know I don't need one. They don't understand that I need to relive it. Nobody understands, so why would a shrink?

Sometimes, when I wake up at night shaking, I get angry at myself for being so scared. I know that I only felt maybe one tenth of the terror that Camille must have felt. She had died alone and scared and hurting. And I got away. I didn't save Camille. And I got away.

I shouldn't have said nobody knows, because Mick does. He's the only one I can stand to be around, practically. We went through it all together. If it wasn't for him, I'd be dead. He said he'd been frantic when he saw the blood on the wall of the locker room. That's when he knew something was wrong. He thought he lost Kristle on the highway, but then he saw the one taillight. He hoped that I had knocked out the light, so he followed the one light through the darkness. But he lost her again after we got off the highway. He drove around for two hours, looking for that car. The police did, too. But Mick was the one who found me.

We don't talk much. He said when I want to talk, I'll talk, and he'll be there. We do corny things, like play gin rummy. And Mick plays piano for me. I thought he just played guitar. He studied classical piano for eight years, and he's really good. He bought me a Mozart CD. And we're talking about maybe going to the symphony in Albany together, which is a seriously strange concept all around.

I think about Kristle a lot. I think about how everybody wants to be loved, and some people think they're unlovable, and then somehow, when they don't get love, they make themselves unlovable. And I wonder if I was heading in that direction.

I lost my best friend, and I got angry, and I hated the world. I hated the life she had without me. I hated all her new friends, even Mick, and I didn't even know him. I was good at the funny remark with the sting underneath. I liked the taste of lemon in my mouth. I liked feeling like the smartest person in the room, the one who was better than everybody else. Maybe part of me even liked being mean.

But not anymore. I'm not as sarcastic as I used to be. I don't make fun of Doug's zits, or Alex's lame basketball playing. Words hurt, you know. And it's like my skin is sensitive to even a raised voice, a harsh word.

Sometimes at night, Mick and I just drive around. We play the radio and don't talk much. If I cry, he doesn't ask me what's wrong. He knows what's wrong. But after a while, he'll reach for my hand and squeeze it. I like feeling his fingers curl through mine.

"What can we do to get over this, Mick?" I asked him on one of those nights we were driving to nowhere. "Is there anything we can do? Not just for us. But for Camille?"

He didn't answer for a while. But I wasn't afraid that he didn't know what I meant.

"I guess we can just remember her," he said finally. "We can remember all the parts we liked. She had a great laugh."

"She made me feel special," I said. "I mean, before she made me feel lousy."

"So that's what we can do for her," Mick said. "We can hold her in our hearts forever. All the parts of her, the good parts and

the bad parts. We can do that much, at least."

Headlights flashed on his face then, turning his golden skin paler than moonlight, pale as bones. I shivered. But then he reached for my hand, and his skin was so warm, and I felt almost cozy, sitting in the car with the night pressing against the windows. And I felt something unfamiliar begin to steal over my face—a smile.

"Yes," I said. "We can do that much."

danger.com

@6//Bad Intent/

by

jordan.cray

1//model school, perfect town

I should fill you in on what happened in our town, Cicada Heights, last year.

The story goes to prove that you can take a handful of boys, pump them full of macho slogans like "Go For It!" and "No Pain, No Gain!" and they'll turn into a pack of rabid wolves.

Basically, four of our All-American football players from the champion Bloomfield High Wolverines went crazy last year. They woke up, pounded their chests, splashed themselves with *eau de testosterone*, and proceeded to torture a handful of their fellow students.

They formed a secret gang called the 24 Point Club. Nobody ever figured out what the name meant, exactly, and the guys weren't talking. On the advice of their very expensive lawyers, so far they've kept their mouths shut.

Here's how it worked. They'd pick a victim, usually a girl. First, they'd steal a personal object, like a glove, or a notebook. Then they'd dye it ʲack and send it to the victim anonymously, with a note saying **SOMEDAY YOU WILL DIE**, and signed, "24 Point Club."

At first, it just seemed like a sick prank. But then Denise Samarian was surrounded in the woods one night and frightened so badly she took off across an icy pond and fell in. No one came to help. She could have drowned, or died from hypothermia, but she got herself out and into her car, driving home with the heater blasting.

Jenny Rigorski was menaced by a group of boys wearing ski masks. Luckily, her father came home before Jenny freaked completely. But then while Megan Malone was babysitting one night, she was tormented by threatening phone calls. She bundled three year old Tyler in her car and took off, crashing into some bushes. No one was hurt, but the investigation turned serious. Put a little kid in danger, and suddenly, everybody gets upset.

Principal Bigelow called about five emergency meetings of the student council and made a bunch of speeches asking anyone with information to come forward. But for once, even the buzzing Bloomfield High gossip mill was silent. Nobody had a clue who these guys were.

Except Coach Cappistrano, who everyone called Cappy. He was the coach of the football team, and not the most swift of individuals. But, in the gym locker room, he found a printout of an e-mail message arranging a meeting. He told th assistant coach that he was suspicious beca

there were no names on the note, only numbers—
the note was headed by the number "2." It was
directed to 8, 9, 3, and 4. He thought maybe it was
code for the 24 Point Club. He was going to show
up at the meeting and try to talk the guys—whoever they were—into giving themselves up.

Coach Cappy went to the rendezvous point, a
parking lot in a park outside of town that had an
outdoor swimming pool, so nobody went there in
winter.   Apparently, all the Wolverine football
heroes were already there—Greg Littlejohn, Kyle
Woodham, David Rollins, and Jamie Fletcher.

Nobody knows what the Coach said, or what
happened. Because they were the last people to see
him alive.

Coach Cappy went back to his house. Later
that night, the doorbell rang. He answered it.

The next thing Cappy knew, he had an extra
nostril. Right between the eyes.

At first, it seemed like a random, shocking act
in a town that hardly bothers to keep crime statis-
tics. Then the cops found the e-mail in Cappy's car,
and the assistant coach told them that the last time
he'd seen him, the coach was heading to a meeting
with the 24 Point Club.

The cops did some pretty impressive TV-show
forensic work. Casts were taken of the tire tracks
on Coach Cappy's lawn. And two footprints were
ound. One was of an expensive athletic shoe. The
er was even more distinctive. They traced it to

a company that made custom-made hiking boots and kept records of people's measurements. That led them to Jamie Fletcher. Listen, if you're going to commit murder, buy your shoes at K-Mart.

The tire tracks matched Kyle's Jeep. A tiny spot of Cappy's blood was found on David's sweatshirt. Greg's Nikes matched the other print. The boys were arrested. They never found the gun. The evidence was circumstantial, but it all added up to a big neon "Guilty!" sign.

None of the guys would talk, except to say that they had formed the club, and things got out of control. They were sorry about that, but they claimed to know nothing about Cappy's murder. Sure, they'd been to his house a bunch of times. And when he'd showed up at the parking lot, he had a nosebleed, and it had gotten on David's shirt. But murder? No way.

All Kyle, Jamie, David, and Greg said was "maybe things got out of hand," and, "I guess some of us used bad judgment."

The district attorney didn't file "bad judgment" charges. He filed Murder One.

Shock rippled through our town. Nobody could believe that our beloved athletes could do such a thing. And there was even some grumbling in town about how fast the cops moved. Couldn't they have waited until *after* football season? They put the championship in jeopardy!

Cicada Heights is an oasis of rationality and

high-mindedness in a world of trivialities.

*We have more golf courses than churches, and
more plastic surgeons than grocers.*

Even after a pile-up of evidence that could be
floated out to sea on a barge, some kids still don't
believe any of the players did it. Greg's old girlfriend, Talia Wilson, was *still* wearing her "Totally
Innocent" T-shirt.

Last year, things got worse when the media got
wind of the story. At first, when the reporters
showed up, everyone was totally impressed. All the
students were dying to be interviewed, and some
guy from the *New York Times* even lived here for
six months to research a book. Up till then,
Bloomfield High had been a major model school.
Smack in the middle of upper middle class subur-
bia, Bloom High boasts every perk a high school
student can possibly crave—computer labs, swimming pool, athletic fields, million dollar football
stadium, in-school TV studio. The school itself
was built in the thirties and completely modern-
ized. A new wing was added just ten years before,
with a system of enclosed catwalks linking the two
buildings.

After the arrests, a black cloud seemed to
descend on the school. We told the world that the
boys didn't represent Bloomfield High. That we
were full of moral, upstanding young citizens. But
nobody seemed to believe us.

Except us.